Readers love the
series by

## *Fire and Flint*

"I cannot recommend this enough. I loved it start to
finish and while it had some super sweet, it was hot
too. So grab your copy and enjoy!"
—Mistress Anya's Reading Nook

"…my sincere recommendation to anyone looking for
a completely fresh story. You'll not regret picking this
one up!"
—*Divine Magazine*

"I love that this series fills me with warmth and strong
love."
—Diverse Reader

## *Fire and Granite*

"Adventure, excitement, fascination, hot sexy times,
danger and so much more is what you will find in this
book. It caught my attention from the start and kept it
all the way to the end."
—MM Good Book Reviews

"*Fire and Granite* is another suspenseful and tension
filled installment in the Carlisle Deputies series. The
plot has plenty of danger and suspicious characters
along with two sweet kids and a cute dog."
—The Novel Approach

"…another great book by Andrew Grey and a great
addition to the series."
—OptimuMM

# By Andrew Grey

Accompanied by a Waltz
All for You
Between Loathing and Love
Borrowed Heart
Buried Passions
Catch of a Lifetime
Chasing the Dream
Crossing Divides
Dominant Chord
Dutch Treat
Eastern Cowboy
Hard Road Back
Half a Cowboy
Heartward
In Search of a Story
Lost and Found
New Tricks
Noble Intentions
North to the Future
One Good Deed
On Shaky Ground
Paint By Number
Past His Defenses
The Playmaker
Pulling Strings
Rebound
Reunited
Running to You
Saving Faithless Creek
Second Go-Round
Shared Revelations
Survive and Conquer
Three Fates
To Have, Hold, and Let Go
Turning the Page
Twice Baked
Unfamiliar Waters
Whipped Cream

ART
Legal Artistry
Artistic Appeal
Artistic Pursuits
Legal Tender

BAD TO BE GOOD
Bad to Be Good
Bad to Be Merry
Bad to Be Noble
Bad to Be Worthy

BOTTLED UP
The Best Revenge
Bottled Up
Uncorked
An Unexpected Vintage

BRONCO'S BOYS
Inside Out
Upside Down
Backward
Round and Round
Over and Back
Above and Beyond

THE BULLRIDERS
A Wild Ride
A Daring Ride
A Courageous Ride

BY FIRE
Redemption by Fire
Strengthened by Fire
Burnished by Fire
Heat Under Fire

Published by DREAMSPINNER PRESS
www.dreamspinnerpress.com

# By ANDREW GREY (cont'd)

**CARLISLE COPS**
Fire and Water
Fire and Ice
Fire and Rain
Fire and Snow
Fire and Hail
Fire and Fog

**CARLISLE DEPUTIES**
Fire and Flint
Fire and Granite
Fire and Agate
Fire and Obsidian
Fire and Onyx
Fire and Diamond

**CARLISLE TROOPERS**
Fire and Sand
Fire and Glass

**CHEMISTRY**
Organic Chemistry
Biochemistry
Electrochemistry
Chemistry Anthology

**DREAMSPUN DESIRES**
The Lone Rancher
Poppy's Secret
The Best Worst
Honeymoon Ever

**EYES OF LOVE**
Eyes Only for Me
Eyes Only for You

**FOREVER YOURS**
Can't Live Without You
Never Let You Go

**GOOD FIGHT**
The Good Fight
The Fight Within
The Fight for Identity
Takoda and Horse

**HEARTS ENTWINED**
Heart Unseen
Heart Unheard
Heart Untouched
Heart Unbroken

**HOLIDAY STORIES**
Copping a Sweetest Day Feel
Cruise for Christmas
A Lion in Tails
Mariah the Christmas Moose
A Present in Swaddling
Clothes
Rudolph the Rescue Jack
Russell
Simple Gifts
Snowbound in Nowhere
Stardust
Sweet Anticipation

**LAS VEGAS ESCORTS**
The Price • The Gift

**LOVE MEANS…**
Love Means… No Shame
Love Means… Courage
Love Means… No Boundaries
Love Means… Freedom
Love Means … No Fear
Love Means… Healing
Love Means… Family
Love Means… Renewal
Love Means… No Limits
Love Means… Patience
Love Means… Endurance

Published by DREAMSPINNER PRESS
www.dreamspinnerpress.com

# By ANDREW GREY (cont'd)

**LOVE'S CHARTER**
Setting the Hook
Ebb and Flow

**MUST LOVE DOGS**
Rescue Me
Rescue Us
Rudolph the Rescue Jack
Russell

**NEW LEAF ROMANCES**
New Leaf
In the Weeds

**PLANTING DREAMS**
Planting His Dream
Growing His Dream

**REKINDLED FLAME**
Rekindled Flame
Cleansing Flame
Smoldering Flame

**SENSES**
Love Comes Silently
Love Comes in Darkness
Love Comes Home
Love Comes Around
Love Comes Unheard
Love Comes to Light

**SEVEN DAYS**
Seven Days
Unconditional Love

**STORIES FROM THE RANGE**
A Shared Range
A Troubled Range
An Unsettled Range
A Foreign Range
An Isolated Range
A Volatile Range
A Chaotic Range

**STRANDED**
Stranded • Taken

**TALES FROM KANSAS**
Dumped in Oz • Stuck in Oz
Trapped in Oz

**TALES FROM ST. GILES**
Taming the Beast
Redeeming the Stepbrother

**TASTE OF LOVE**
A Taste of Love
A Serving of Love
A Helping of Love
A Slice of Love

**WITHOUT BORDERS**
A Heart Without Borders
A Spirit Without Borders

**WORK OUT**
Spot Me • Pump Me Up
Core Training • Crunch Time
Positive Resistance
Personal Training
Cardio Conditioning
Work Me Out Anthology

Published by DREAMSPINNER PRESS
www.dreamspinnerpress.com

# FIRE AND AGATE
# ANDREW GREY

DREAMSPINNER PRESS

Published by
DREAMSPINNER PRESS

5032 Capital Circle SW, Suite 2, PMB# 279,
Tallahassee, FL 32305-7886 USA
www.dreamspinnerpress.com

Fire and Agate
© 2018 Andrew Grey

Cover Art
© 2018 Kanaxa
kanaxa@gmail.com
Cover content is for illustrative purposes only and any person depicted
on the cover is a model.

Mass Market Paperback ISBN: 978-1-64108-490-1
Trade Paperback ISBN: 978-1-64080-943-7
Digital ISBN: 978-1-64080-942-0
Mass Market Paperback published April 2023
v. 1.0

Printed in the United States of America
∞
This paper meets the requirements of
ANSI/NISO Z39.48-1992 (Permanence of Paper)

*To Chris,*
*for helping me with all the researchand giving me*
*hope that this story could actually work.*

# CHAPTER 1

"CHRIS," BRIGGS said as he stalked into the locker room like a man on a mission. His gaze was hard and his posture as rigid as a two-by-four. Anger and discontent rolled off him in waves, worse than Chris had ever seen in the month since he had moved from jail duty.

Two years of whining, demanding prisoners who thought being in jail was the worst thing to ever happen to them and thought a jail cell should be like a suite at the Hilton. Those were the ones Chris was pretty sure were never going to see the inside of a cell again if they could help it. And then there were the repeat offenders who thought of the jail as home and a chance at three meals a day. God, he had hated every minute of the constant noise of men and women talking, fighting, yammering on about nothing just to make noise so the reality of the shit they were in didn't close in around them.

"What can I do for you?" Chris smiled as best he could. Briggs had been instrumental in getting him off jail duty and into the sheriff's office, so he owed the guy.

"It's not me. His Majesty wants to see you." Briggs turned, flashing a beam of damn near hatred out the door.

Not that Chris blamed the guy. When Sheriff Hunter had decided to retire, Briggs had stepped in as acting sheriff at Hunter's request. The entire department had been pretty happy about it. Briggs was well respected and good at his job. But the county board had other ideas. They did some lame-assed search, and lo and behold, they'd found the current sheriff, a political appointee. That had been a month ago, but Briggs still hadn't gotten over it.

"Thanks." He checked that his uniform was perfect, because that was what Sheriff Mario Vitalli liked. He was all about how things looked and appeared. It didn't seem to matter how things got done as long as he looked good—at least that was the general feeling in the locker room. "I'll go right away."

Briggs rolled his eyes. "He's on a call, so give him five minutes."

Vitalli liked everyone to wait for him, though he never wanted to wait for anyone or anything. Which would be fine if he were good at his job. He wasn't particularly—at least Chris didn't think so.

"Okay." Chris wanted to say something to Briggs. He really thought a lot of him, but everything that came to mind sounded completely lame, so he kept quiet and showed Briggs the respect he thought he deserved.

"Do you want something?" Briggs asked, taking a step closer.

Chris realized he'd sunk into his thoughts and had been looking at nothing in particular. Briggs must have thought he was staring at him. "No." Chris turned away and closed his locker. "I'll see you around." He left the room and headed up to where the big guy had his office.

The door was closed, so Chris sat in the chair outside to wait. Things had changed a lot in a month. Everyone was quiet around the office. The people who worked near the sheriff all spoke in whispers. Sheriff

Vitalli didn't like noise, and to him, talking meant people weren't working. Which seemed ridiculous to Chris, because for him, talking in a sheriff's office meant work was getting done and investigations were being discussed and moving forward.

The door opened and Sheriff Vitalli tilted his head outside.

Chris snapped to his feet, went in, and closed the door. "Good morning."

"Anducci," Vitalli said, taking his seat behind the desk. Chris couldn't miss the file that sat there in front of him, and wondered if he was being sent back to the jail. His stomach clenched. He'd worked hard and diligently to get out of there. "I have an assignment for you." He pushed the file off to the side as though he had made a decision. Chris wondered if it was good or bad.

"Yes, sir," he said quietly, hoping to hell he wasn't on his way back. No matter what, he was going to have to return to his locker for an antacid.

Vitalli shook his head and scoffed. "Everyone seems to think that this office is some kind of protection service." He sneered.

Chris kept his mouth shut. It *was* their job to protect the public, which was why they became police officers in the first place. At least why Chris had. Granted, most people would think him idealistic, but so the fuck what.

"Are you listening?"

"Yes," Chris answered quickly.

"I got a request from a social worker." Vitalli yanked open a drawer and pulled out a thin file, then tossed it on the desk dramatically. "The cops in Carlisle busted up a whorehouse and found a bunch of aliens working there. In their touchy-feely world, they set about helping them and found they were brought here against their will." He rolled his eyes. "I'm not buying it, but no one asked me my opinion. Anyway, they say they need help for one person they found. It's a man, not a woman...." The sheriff paused as if he were expecting some sort of agreement to his ignorance and shortsightedness. He didn't seem to believe that men could be trafficked as well as women, and Chris wasn't going to agree with him.

"Human trafficking takes many forms," Chris said, then cleared his throat when the sheriff frowned deeply. "What would you like me to do?"

Vitalli groaned dramatically. "The Social Services folks found these people safe places to live, but one of them has been found out. Apparently he's preparing to testify against his captors, and now he's been getting threats. The feds, DA, and Social Services are all asking for protection for this guy, and it's falling on me to provide it. So...." He picked up the file and thrust it toward Chris. "It's you."

"Me?" He took the file and tucked it under his arm. He wasn't going to read it while standing in front of the sheriff.

"Can we not let this interfere with your shifts?" he groused, then turned back to his empty desk, grabbing the first piece of paper he could find.

"Is there anything else?"

He didn't think he was going to get an answer, but then the sheriff lifted his gaze. "Don't screw this up. It's an easy job, so just do it and be done." He turned away, back to his papers. Chris took it as a dismissal and left the office, closing the door behind him.

With a sigh of relief, Chris went to his old metal desk at the back of the station and placed the file on the empty surface. He was usually out on patrol or working with one of the other deputies, so he spent very little time there. No pictures or papers littered the space, just a phone and a few files hanging in one of the drawers. It would be so easy for him to pack up and move on. Part of him, some fear deep inside, wondered how long he would get to stay before being sent back to jail duty.

"What did the sheriff want?" Pierre asked as he approached the desk.

"He gave me an assignment," Chris said, rather pleased.

Pierre smiled. "It looks like you're going to stay, then." Pierre had been the first one to welcome him, handing over a fresh coffee on Chris's first day. "That's good."

"Suppose so, as long as I don't mess it up." Chris opened the file and scanned through it. There wasn't much information, just a name and address for the witness, along with information on how to contact the caseworker. "Kasun, Pavle Kasun…," he said, and nodded.

"Does that mean anything to you?" Pierre asked.

"Not personally. My mother's family is Serbian, and this has that sound." He picked up the phone and called the number for the caseworker. It went to voicemail, so he left a message asking her to call back as soon as she was able.

"What did the sheriff tell you?"

"That this Pavle is a witness who was in a safe house until he was found out. I suspect he's been moved, and they want me to try to help keep him safe until the FBI and DA can talk to him and he can testify against the traffickers." It shouldn't be too difficult a job as long as they could keep his location a secret.

"Then do what you can for him." Pierre glanced at the sheriff's office, choosing his words carefully. "He doesn't think too much of others… who are different. Anyone who is different from him."

"I see." Chris knew Pierre had a partner, Jordan, who worked at the courthouse, and there were other gay men in the department. Apparently they were worried about this particular sheriff. Sheriff Hunter hadn't been prejudiced; either that or he hadn't cared as long as the job got done. Chris supposed that was probably the best kind of person to occupy the office. Someone who looked at accomplishments and results.

"No, you don't. Be careful, and do this to the best of your ability." Pierre clapped Chris on the shoulder. "Because this could be your one and only chance with this man. He doesn't seem to abide anything that makes him look bad in any way." Pierre held his gaze, and Chris nodded. They were both thinking of Graves, who the new sheriff had already demoted and relegated to patrolling country roads for speeding and crap just because one of his arrests fell through on procedural grounds.

"I know." Chris had started reviewing the file again when his phone rang. He smiled at Pierre, who left his desk, and Chris answered the call.

"Hello, this is Marie Foster returning your call. Is this in regards to Pavle?" She sounded tired, like she hadn't slept or had a break in weeks.

"Yes. I was hoping I could meet you and we could discuss what you believe is required, and then I'd like to meet him. I need to assess the situation so I can develop a plan to help keep him safe."

"Excellent. If you'd like to come to my office on Pitt Street, we can go see him from there." She gave him the address. "And please don't come in an official car. We don't want to draw attention to where he is. This is the third safe house we've housed him at, and we keep getting indications that he's been found. We don't know how, and I don't want to take any chances."

"Then I'll change into civilian clothes as well before I come see you."

"Thank you. I'll see you in about half an hour, then."

After hanging up, Chris left his desk, picking up the file to take it with him. He returned to the locker area, changed out of his uniform, and let dispatch know that he was going to be out on an assignment from the sheriff. Then he took his own car and drove the five minutes to the office.

The building embodied small and utilitarian at its worst—nothing at all of any personality in the place— and Marie's office was equally drab and stuck in the eighties. When he entered, she stood to offer her hand. Then he sat in an olive-green office chair that creaked under his weight.

Marie was a big woman with a ready smile and bright, expressive eyes that bristled with intelligence and care. She dressed professionally casual, wearing a dark blue and white blouse with jeans. Her office was as neat and organized as any he'd seen. Two phones rested in holders on her desk, which also held a computer and a few pictures.

"Why don't you tell me what's going on so I can try to help?" Chris asked, needing to get some background.

She nodded. "We discovered the house about three weeks ago, and the Carlisle Police raided the place. They discovered people inside, including two wanted sex offenders, who are still in custody in the county prison, and Pavle, who was cowering in the corner of a closet. It took them an hour to get him to come out. Once they called me, I was able to explain enough to him that he understood those people were there to help him."

"Did you work with him?"

"Yes. I found him a safe house that was a group home with five other individuals. It was... not good. He cowered when any men came near him and basically stayed in a corner, watching everyone, for days. Either that or he went to his room and hid. I think his poor mind was simply overloaded. Then someone tried to set fire to the home and damaged it enough that everyone had to be relocated. That was hard, but then they reported people watching the next house two days after Pavle moved in." She swallowed and leaned back in her chair.

"Do you think someone is feeding his captors information?" Chris asked.

"Honestly? Yes," she said, and he nodded. "We have a system that tracks each person in our safe houses. Pavle has been anonymized, but someone is using the information to try to find him, which is a violation of a number of state and federal laws." Marie leaned forward, her demeanor turning more serious. "We can't protect him anymore, and the longer he stays in the safe house, the more he and the others there with him are in danger." She humphed softly. "At the moment he's being housed in a home for women because we didn't want to put him with men right now. And that's causing some problems for the women, though I think those are dissipating." She was clearly coming to the end of her resources. "I guess what I'm asking you is if you'd be willing to take Pavle to live with you. That way I can remove him from the system, at least as far as the information about where he's staying. Get him off the grid for a while."

That hadn't been something Chris had thought about doing, and the request surprised him. His instinct was to say no. His own home was his sanctuary, and he liked to keep it that way. Growing up, he'd moved many times—military family. Luckily, when his dad had been close to retirement, he'd been able to get posted to the Carlisle Barracks, near family. Chris's home here was like his castle because it was the first one he'd had that was his and no one else's.

"Why don't you take me to meet him and then we can see what we need to do," Chris said, purposely vague and noncommittal. Surely Marie couldn't blame him for not giving an answer until he met Pavle.

"I'll do that. But there are some things you need to know first." She floundered, seeming to be trying to figure out where to start. "We haven't gotten the full story from him about how he got here. There is a language barrier that's hard for us to breach. He does speak some English, mostly what he taught himself from listening to his captors and the few people he's been around for the last four years."

Chris gaped. How in the hell could someone live that way for such a long time? "Oh my God."

"Yes. We believe he was brought in through New Jersey during the Super Bowl in 2014. Newark is a huge human trafficking point of entry. Anyway, we aren't sure how long he's been in Carlisle or how many owners he's had over the years."

Her words sent a spike through Chris's heart. How in the hell could people do that to someone else? Chris had most definitely seen human beings at their lowest, and just when he thought he'd seen it all… *wham*… it got worse.

"Okay. So he's been traumatized and most likely gaslighted for years," he said, and Marie nodded. "So in his mind, this is all his fault, and everything that has happened to him is because of something he did."

"You got it. Years of fear and guilt conditioning. Those are the greatest weapons they have. Though, deep down, there is some steel in his back. There has to be for him to have survived this long." She gathered her purse and phone, as well as a spring jacket. The early May weather this year had been up and down. "This is the address." She handed it to him on a small sheet of notepaper, and Chris memorized it and dropped it into the shredder in the corner of the office. That earned him a smile.

"I'll meet you there. I'm in the blue Edge," he explained as he left the office with Marie behind him.

Inside the car, he took a few minutes to breathe. Things like this shouldn't affect him. He saw bad things every day. But this story got under his skin, and he needed a few minutes to get his professional distance back into place. Once his anger and indignation wore down a little, he pulled out of the lot and drove to the east side of town. He parked on the street and waited for Marie before approaching the house with her.

Marie stopped at the base of the walk. "I know you're a cop, but try not to walk like one. You're standing tall and strong. I know in your job you have to project strength, but here that's not a benefit. Every one of these people have been abused or hurt at the hands of a man, so they are going to be intimidated."

Chris slumped a little and lowered his gaze slightly. "Better?"

"Try smiling and not being so serious."

Chris chuckled, and Marie must have approved because she turned, continued forward, and knocked on the door.

The house was deadly silent. Three women sat in chairs, looking up at him as though he were the devil incarnate, fear radiating off each and every one of them. He nodded to each lady and gave them all a small smile.

"This is Deputy Chris," Marie said.

"What he want?" one of the ladies asked. She had big brown eyes, and her lips curled in a sneer.

"Letty, that's enough," Marie said gently, but with a firm undertone. "He's here to help Pavle."

A woman bustled into the room, and Marie introduced her as the housemother, Annette.

"His room is down the hall. He rarely leaves it, even to eat," Annette explained, never raising her voice much above a whisper. "Follow me." She turned to lead him down the hallway to the last room. Annette knocked, spoke softly, and opened the door.

The curtains were drawn, the room dark, even though it was the middle of the day. A single light burned next to a twin bed that had been made to within an inch of its life, with corners sharp enough to make any drill sergeant proud. The room, however, was empty.

"Pavle, sweetheart. It's Annette," she said gently and waited.

Slowly a figure, curled up and small, made an appearance from around the side of the dresser. The first thing Chris noticed were the biggest, brownest eyes he had ever seen, filled with the pain of years of hurt. They blinked, and then Pavle stepped farther into the light. Even standing, he looked half hunched over.

"This is Deputy Chris. He's here because he's going to help keep you safe."

Pavle raised his head slightly, his black hair, long and uneven, falling to the sides of his face.

"Hello," Chris said, mimicking the soft tone the others had used. "I'm Chris. They told me you needed help, so I'm going to protect you so no one hurts you anymore." In that moment, he made up his mind to do whatever was needed to help this man, and if that meant moving him into his home to protect him, so be it.

"I'd like it if you went with Deputy Chris. He is a good man and will not hurt you," Marie explained slowly and gently.

Chris didn't expect Pavle to believe her or to agree to come. "It's okay if you don't want to," Chris said, crouching down so he was at the same level as Pavle. "This is your choice."

"Choice?" Pavle asked in a raspy voice that tore at Chris's insides, looking at him and then back to Marie.

"Yes. You can choose to stay here or go with Deputy Chris. We want you to be safe, but we aren't sure how well we can protect you here. If you go with Deputy Chris, he will protect you. Keep you safe."

"INS?" Pavle asked.

"No. He is good man. Caring. He will help you." Marie seemed to have infinite patience.

Pavle blinked, standing still, then nodded and walked to Chris. It seemed as though he either didn't understand or thought he didn't have a choice, even though he was being given one. Chris held out his hands, palms up, to show that he wasn't going to hit him. When Pavle looked at him with those huge eyes and the face of an angel, he looked much younger than the twenty-four listed in his file. Maybe that was his previous owner's fetish. Still, after all he'd been through, Pavle's handsomeness and light shone through, with soft features and an almost delicate frame.

"I'll gather his few things," Annette said.

Marie extended her hand to take Pavle's gently. He went with her in silence. She led him out of the house, and once they were in the sun, Chris got a better look at him. Pavle was pale, probably from years of being inside. Chris reminded himself to ask Marie about any past injuries. He suspected that Pavle had been treated very badly in the past and he needed to know if he was okay physically.

"Thank you for doing this," Marie said once she had opened the door to Chris's car and gotten Pavle settled in the passenger seat. He sat without moving or looking to either side. "You have to keep him safe. He is the main witness against the man who held him for nearly two years. We need to get that man and then trace back to the people who sold Pavle to him. We're pulling each thread to see what we can unravel."

"Okay. I will do my best, I promise you."

"I'll follow you to your house and help Pavle get settled."

As Marie got to her car, Pavle reacted for the first time.

"She's just riding separately. She will be back in a few minutes."

Chris drove the short distance to his house and pulled into the garage. He didn't want Pavle to be seen, and yet he also didn't want him to feel like a prisoner again by being hidden. He got out and waited, hoping Pavle would get out on his own. After a few moments, Pavle opened the door and climbed out of the car. Chris opened the door to the yard and motioned for Pavle to go ahead of him.

Marie came through behind him, and Chris closed the garage doors and joined the two of them in the yard. Pavle looked around, saying nothing. Chris wished he would say something… anything. He was way too quiet, and that worried Chris because he had no idea what he was thinking, and damn it all, those eyes still held buckets of fear.

"It's okay. This is where you are going to stay." Marie gently coaxed Pavle toward the house, and he shuffled along, looking at the yard. Hopefully he liked what he saw. Chris had spent too many hours working out stress for the garden to be unappreciated.

Chris opened the back door, went inside, and turned on lights, letting Marie bring Pavle into the kitchen, motioning toward the living room. Maybe this was the biggest mistake of his life. He wasn't equipped to handle someone as fragile and frightened as Pavle. Chris had no clue what he needed or even how to get through to him.

"I sold?" Pavle finally asked, barely above a whisper.

Chris caught Marie's gaze, and his heart twisted in his chest. God, this was going to wrench his guts six ways from Sunday.

"No. This is where you are going to live. You are not going to be sold to anyone anymore. Deputy Chris is here to help you and nothing more." She patted his hand and took Pavle through to the other room.

Chris got three glasses of water and put some cookies on a plate. He needed some sugar if he was going to get through this in one piece.

Marie and Pavle were talking softly on the sofa when Chris handed each of them a glass and offered them cookies. Marie took one, and Pavle stared at the plate as though it were a foreign object. Finally, he took one and ate a small bite before shoving the whole thing in his mouth, chewing and swallowing like he hadn't eaten in days. Then he drank the entire glass of water.

Chris offered him another, and Pavle took it in disbelief, ate it quickly, and then rested his hands in his lap.

"Why don't I take you upstairs and show you your room?" Chris offered. He led Pavle and Marie upstairs and into the bright guest room, with cream walls and a deep green coverlet on the bed. The furniture was white and rather plain, but functional. He'd found the set at a secondhand store and painted it himself to clean it up. "You can put your clothes in here," Chris told Pavle, who shrugged and looked down at what he was wearing.

"I have his things in the car. There isn't much right now," Marie explained.

"That's okay. I can take him to get everything he needs." Chris needed to do some shopping tomorrow anyway and figured he could take Pavle with him. He would need to disguise Pavle somehow. "I have something he can wear tonight if he needs to, and then we'll shop tomorrow."

"Thank you," Marie said with a sigh. "Are you going to be okay?" she asked Pavle, who nodded.

Chris showed her downstairs, while Pavle stayed behind, and got Pavle's things from her car.

"I'll stop by whenever I can. He's going to need care and plenty of help."

"Of course. Is he seeing a counselor?" Chris asked.

"Yes. But they are having some language issues. I'm working on it. I'd like to find one who understands Serbian so they can talk in his native language, but it's very difficult in this area. But I'm not giving up. I'll let you know when his next appointment is." She left through the back gate, and Chris locked it from the inside and went back into the house. He brought Pavle's things up to his room and set them on the bed next to him.

"Are you hungry?" Chris asked. When Pavle finally nodded, Chris motioned, and they left the room. He didn't know what to make for dinner, but decided on pasta. He got Pavle seated in the kitchen and started cooking. It wasn't fancy, and the sauce was from a jar, but when he put the plate and a glass of water in front of Pavle, the surprised expression and then the way he shoveled the food into his mouth, his arm nearly a blur, told him a great deal about Pavle's treatment. Chris got his attention and ate slowly. "I'm not going to take your food."

Pavle nodded and ate a little more leisurely, but his body was rigid the entire time, as if he expected Chris to take away his plate at any moment.

Once Pavle had eaten everything, Chris got him a little more and showed Pavle what he had to drink. Pavle pointed, and Chris poured him some juice. Pavle sniffed the glass and sipped before downing the liquid like it was a huge shot.

"I am not going to take your food or drink. You can have all you want." He poured Pavle some more grape juice and set it in front of him before clearing the dishes. Pavle stared at the glass like it held some deep meaning and then sighed dramatically and drank it.

Once Chris had cleaned up, he motioned for Pavle to follow him through to the living room. Chris put on the television and sat in the chair. Pavle sat in the other one, alternately watching the television and then him. It was a little unnerving, but Chris sat still and tried to relax, hoping Pavle would do the same.

At bedtime, he turned off the television and led Pavle up the stairs, turning out the lights. "It's time to go to bed." He showed Pavle the bathroom and the towels that were his to use. He also found a new toothbrush and some extra toiletries for him, placing them on the bathroom counter. He tried to think of anything he was forgetting. "Is there anything else you need?"

Pavle shook his head and went to his room, and when Chris came in to bring him some pajamas, Pavle stood in the center of the room, naked, his hands behind his back, head bent down.

# CHAPTER 2

CHRIS STOOD stunned into inaction. He hadn't been expecting this at all, not for a moment. And Pavle was breathtaking. Chris's brain instantly clicked on to the gorgeousness, damn near perfection, standing in front of him. So yeah, he looked for a second, and then rationality kicked in.

"No," he whispered and turned away, giving Pavle some privacy. "Please put these on. I…." He swallowed as heat rose to his cheeks. Damn, this was a fucking minefield. "That is not what you're here for." He held out the soft nightclothes, and Pavle reached for them. He slowly pulled them on as though he thought Chris might be crazy. Once Pavle was covered, Chris motioned for him to sit on the edge of the bed. "This is your room. You are not here for sex. You stay here, and I keep you safe until you have to go to court and testify." God, he hoped Pavle understood some of this.

Pavle blinked up at him with those huge, stunning eyes, and Chris sighed, rubbing his eyes as he willed his heart to return to normal.

"I use bathroom," Pavle finally said, and after Chris nodded his understanding, he left the room.

Chris swallowed hard and went to his own room, leaving the door open so he could hear if Pavle needed help. The toilet flushed and water ran, leaving Chris feeling like a voyeur of sorts, but he wasn't sure what would happen next. When Pavle came out, he crossed to his room, and after a few seconds, the bed squeaked and that was all.

Chris took a turn in the bathroom, noting that Pavle had used the toothbrush. Hell, other than a very few indications, it was like he'd never been in the room. He thought of asking Pavle if he wanted to take a shower, but had second thoughts, fearing Pavle would think he wanted to take one with him and….

He cleaned up and turned out the bathroom light. Across the hall, Chris could see a figure curled up in the bed in Pavle's room. Chris didn't know why, but he felt tension radiating out from him, like even at rest, Pavle was on guard. He hoped with time that Pavle would begin to trust him and that things would get better.

Chris went to his room, leaving the door ajar so he could hear Pavle in the night, and crawled into bed. He found himself listening for a while but heard no sound from Pavle and eventually fell asleep, though he didn't get a lot of rest.

After tossing and turning once the morning light hit the windows in his room, he got up and went downstairs. He started the coffee, then sat at the table with a mug and his laptop to read the morning news and to sign in to the department so he could check the logs just to see what was going on. He'd probably been at it an hour when his stomach rumbled, so he started breakfast.

A scent, soft and slightly musky, gave the first indication that he wasn't alone. He hadn't heard Pavle come down, even on the squeaky stairs of the century-and-a-half-old row house.

"Would you like some coffee?" Chris poured a mug and offered it to Pavle, who took it and sipped.

Pavle sighed, and Chris smiled to himself, willing his mind to remember that, the first sound of contentment of any type Chris had heard from him.

"I'm making breakfast." Chris put a pan of bacon in the oven and started working on some eggs and toast. "Do you want some juice?"

Pavle nodded. "Yes, thank you," he said warily, watching him. Pavle watched everything he did, each and every second.

Once the food was ready, Chris placed the plates and utensils, along with juice glasses and some fresh fruit, on a tray and carried it outside. He loved to eat on the patio. Once he set the tray on the table, he turned to find that Pavle hadn't followed him. Pavle stood in the kitchen doorway, looking outside but not moving.

"Oh my God," Chris whispered to himself, wondering when the last time had been that Pavle had stayed outside during the day… or at any time. "You can come out," he said, louder.

Pavle took a step outside, turning his head upward and closing his eyes as the sun shone on his face. He simply stood there as though rediscovering the sun.

"Are you hungry?" Chris asked softly, and Pavle nodded after a second. He walked over, his head craning from side to side. Chris indicated the chair, and Pavle sat down but didn't eat. "That's yours," Chris said, and started eating.

"I no understand," Pavle said.

Chris paused and set down his fork. "Tell me. You can talk all you like. Talk to me." God, he was trying to infer what Pavle thought and felt from his actions and inactions, and it was hard as hell.

"I no…," Pavle started, breathing rapidly. "You… last night…." Agitation rang in his voice. Chris wanted nothing more than to take him in his arms to comfort him, but didn't dare.

"What about last night?" Chris asked.

Pavle's eyes swirled with confusion and doubt. Chris waited patiently, letting Pavle think about what he wanted to say. "You no… I have to pay, and…."

Chris shook his head slowly. "No. You don't have to pay. Marie and I are helping you, and we want nothing in return." He tapped Pavle's plate. "You eat all you want. And you don't have to pay me back." He was so tempted to take Pavle's hand to comfort him, but he resisted. "Those days are over. Your body is your own, and no one is going to make you pay for things with it. Not me, not Marie." Now he hoped Pavle understood. "Go ahead and eat." He smiled, and Pavle picked up his fork, digging into the food.

Chris finished his breakfast and put his dishes on the tray. Pavle drank his juice and smacked his lips. When Chris took his dishes inside, he brought the bottle and refilled Pavle's glass. Pavle looked up at him as though wondering what Chris wanted from him, but Chris decided to ignore the look. He'd also brought the coffeepot and refilled his mug and topped off Pavle's.

Today was his day off, so at least he wasn't going to have to figure out what to do with Pavle while he was gone, not until Friday when he was back on shift. That gave him a couple of days. His phone chimed and he picked it up off the table. He answered Marie's text, saying they were doing okay and he was going to take Pavle to the store to get him some clothes. He hoped that was a good idea.

*I'll bring over some vouchers. What store are you going to?*

*Target,* he answered, and Marie said she'd be around in half an hour. *Great. See you then. He set his phone aside.*

Pavle had finished eating and was actually leaning back in his chair. "Thank you. It good." He took his time pronouncing the words, clearly trying to improve his language skills. He smiled, though it seemed a little forced.

"I'm glad you liked it." Chris gathered the last of the dishes. "I'm going to take these inside. You can stay out here if you want." He carried in the dishes and loaded the dirty ones into the dishwasher. A soft scrape reached his ears, and Chris opened the door to the back sitting room and peered out the window. Pavle had moved his chair over a little, sitting with the sun shining on him. He looked angelic like that, his head back and eyes closed.

A knock caught his attention, and Chris went to the front door to let Marie inside.

"How is he doing?"

Chris briefly told her about the incident last evening. "I explained things to him, I hope."

"That's not unexpected. Pavle is used to paying for his food, his bed, everything, with his body. It was the only currency he had." Marie sighed, opened her bag, and handed Chris an envelope. "I brought some cards for Giant as well. That way at least we're helping with groceries too." She flashed a quick smile. "How much do you know about his situation… human trafficking in general?" she asked as Chris motioned her through the house.

"Not a lot. It was discussed in the academy, but this is my first real exposure." He continued to the back room. Pavle hadn't moved a muscle, just sat still in the sun. "I think he likes being outside."

"Probably because he hasn't been outside for most of the last four years, at least until his rescue. He was brought in for the Super Bowl, as I said. It's all organized crime, the big families. They bring them in, and once they're through customs, they tell them that they need to have their passports specially checked. They take their papers, and then they're stuck. Pavle was probably told he had to work off the cost of his transportation and everything else before they would give him his documents back. Once the Super Bowl was over, he was most likely sold and eventually ended up here. He was always someone's dirty secret, so he was never outside and always kept hidden. It's all he knows." Marie pulled a tissue out of her purse and blew her nose. "I've seen a ton of shit, but this always gets to me."

"How long will he stay out there?" Chris asked.

"My guess is until you get him. See, right now, I think he's soaking in the sun because he thinks it's all going to be taken away." She gasped slightly. "I forgot something in the car." She hurried away, and Chris followed her to wait at the front door. She returned with a Kohl's bag. "I got him some clothes." She handed him the bag. "Leave the tags on them when you give them to him. He needs to know they're new. That they are for him and not hand-me-downs."

"Why don't you give them to him?" Chris asked, handing her back the bag.

"Because he needs to trust someone other than me." Marie passed it back. "Now let's go talk to him."

Pavle jumped when they came outside and hurried to put the chair back in its original place.

"It's okay. You can leave the chair there." Chris smiled, and Pavle put the chair back where it had been, then sat on the edge of it.

"Hi, Pavle. We brought you a few things," Marie said.

Chris handed him the bag, and Pavle set it on the paving stones. He pulled out the jeans and a light green polo shirt, as well as some underwear and socks, all in packages and with tags. "New?" he asked, and damn it all if he didn't hug the jeans to his chest as though they were precious. Chris shared a look with Marie and wondered if he was ever going to understand what motivated Pavle to do that. "For me?"

"Yes. And Chris is going to take you to get some more clothes." She handed Pavle a piece of paper. "I have set up some appointments with a teacher who is going to help you with English and writing." She took his hand. "We are here to help you and to try to see if we can guide you to build a good life. Do you understand?"

"Yes. I no pay. Mister no hurt anymore." He blinked, and Marie nodded slowly. "Annette say my body mine now."

"That's right. You don't belong to anyone but you." Marie smiled, and Chris did the same, nodding, relieved.

"I have to go to the store to get some food. Do you want to come with me?" Chris asked, wanting to be clear that Pavle could decide. "We can also stop and get you some more clothes."

"More?" Pavle asked.

"Yes. We want you to have enough for three or four days," Marie told him. "Is there anything you need?"

Pavle hesitated and then shook his head before turning to Chris. "Can we get… juice?"

Chris snickered slightly. "Yes. There are lots of different kinds, and you can choose what you like." He shook his head, looking at Marie. "Pavle has discovered that he likes grape juice." Chris figured he'd buy a case of the stuff if it was what Pavle wanted.

Marie smiled. "I need to go back to the office. I'm supposed to man it this afternoon. But call me if you need anything, and I will do my best to help." She said goodbye, and Chris let her out the front door, closing and locking it behind her. He didn't want Pavle to think he was being held prisoner again, but he also wanted him to be safe, so locking up was a necessity.

"What is that?" Pavle asked, pointing to a number of plants Chris intended to put in the ground. The garden club had held their annual plant sale a week ago, but he hadn't had a chance to get them planted yet. That had been something he wanted to do today.

"Those are flowers. I want to plant them." He turned to Pavle, who seemed interested. "Do you want to help?" Maybe this was a way to help break some of the ice between them.

Pavle nodded slowly, a little nervously.

"Okay. I'll get the tools, and we can do it together." Chris got small shovels and a rake, setting them aside before placing each of the pots where he wanted it. Then he got a tub for the dirt and showed Pavle how to dig the hole and set the plant in, loosening the soil in the tub before filling the hole once again. The plants he had were pretty hardy, and he offered the shovel to Pavle, who started on the next plant.

Chris watched him out of the corner of his eye as Pavle dug the most exacting hole in the history of gardening and then carefully set the plant inside after removing it from the pot. "Is good?"

"Yes. It's very good," Chris praised, and got the watering can to give each of the plants a drink before moving on.

"I like," Pavle said, moving to the next plant.

Chris half watched him as he worked. Pavle concentrated so much on each thing he did that Chris wondered just what caused that attention to detail. Had he been punished if things weren't exactly right? He wished he could ask Pavle about his previous life, but then again, the Carlisle Police had already asked him a ton of questions, and he knew the state police were next on the list, and then the FBI once they got around to it. Marie had told him that there was even the possibility that Interpol might get involved. Pavle was going to have to tell his story to plenty of people before this was over, and Chris didn't want him to do anything he didn't want to.

"What are?" Pavle asked, pointing to a stack of plastic bags next to the garage.

"Mulch." Chris reached over and scooped up some of the shredded wood that he'd already put down. "We put it around the plants to help hold in the water. I'll show you when we have everything in the ground."

He and Pavle planted the remaining dozen flowers and watered them in. Chris showed Pavle how to spread the mulch, and then they were done. The garden had been freshened up with new blooms and some color.

"You happy?" Pavle asked.

"Yes. Are you?" Chris watched as confusion warred on Pavle's face. Maybe he hadn't liked the gardening, and what Chris thought might have been fun was just another awful thing someone had made Pavle do.

"I like." Then Pavle held up his hands, and Chris understood his question.

"We'll wash up once we put the tools away. Then we can change into clean clothes. You can try on your new ones, and we can go to the store."

Once they had everything put away, they went inside. Pavle went upstairs, and Chris heard him in the bathroom. He was taking quite a while.

After locking up the back, Chris went up and found Pavle dressed in his new clothes, the ones he'd worn hanging wet in the bathroom. "I have a washing machine," he said as gently as he could because he didn't want to scold him. He figured Pavle had spent years washing his own clothes any way he could. "We can use that to wash clothes. You don't have to do it yourself like that. When we come back, I'll show you." He left the laundry where it was because he didn't want Pavle to feel bad. He had a feeling there were going to be a lot of surprises in his future, and Chris needed to watch for each and every one of them. It was becoming pretty clear that Pavle had had no exposure to American life the entire time he'd been here, and it was going to be up to him to help introduce Pavle to things a little at a time.

SHOPPING WITH Pavle was a unique experience. When Chris took him to Target, Pavle stepped into the store and froze right near the corral of red carts, staring. His mouth hung open, and he pressed to Chris, shaking, as a large group of people came in.

"It's all right. They are just here to shop too."

"Anybody come here?" Pavle asked.

Chris nodded. "Yes. This is a store for everyone. All stores are." He pulled a cart out of the stack. "Why don't we look around and you can pick out some clothes for yourself?"

Pavle put his hands to his chest. "Me choose?" he asked, then broke into another smile. "Okay. I like choose." Pavle picked out shirts in bright, almost wild colors, two more pairs of jeans, and even orange socks. At first Chris thought Pavle was color-blind, but then he realized that he was just getting what he liked. His world had been drab for a long time, and now it was brightening up.

After their adventure in Target, the grocery store was a completely different experience. Pavle couldn't believe there was so much food. He walked into the brightly lit store, stopped, stared, and then tears ran down his cheeks. His left hand shook, and Chris hoped he wasn't having a stroke. He was prepared to get Pavle out of there when Pavle turned to him.

"Where so much food from?" He wiped his eyes.

"This is how food stores are here," Chris said gently. "There's a bakery section over there for bread, and there are fresh fruits and vegetables." He wasn't sure how much Pavle was understanding, so he showed him through the entire store, taking his time and letting him see everything.

"Everyone here is rich," Pavle commented, wide-eyed. "So much… everything."

Chris texted Marie and told her where they were and Pavle's reaction.

She messaged him back quickly. *That's a normal reaction. Let him see everything, let him pick out fresh things. He probably has had nothing at all since he came here. Please just give him choices and let him taste. Take it slow, and if he gets overwhelmed, be prepared to leave.*

Chris thanked her and let Pavle wander. He seemed fascinated with the fresh fruit, lifting oranges and apples, caressing them as though they were gold, and then gingerly putting them back.

"Do you want those?"

Pavle bit his lower lip. "How pay?" he whispered.

"Marie gave me money to get things for you. We can get them." Chris smiled and grabbed some of the oranges that Pavle had been fascinated with, as well as some of the apples. They picked out vegetables and cheeses, along with bread and other things that Pavle seemed interested in. And, of course, juice of every flavor and color.

When he got back home, Chris was starving. He put the groceries away, and made them a late sandwich lunch, which Pavle ate quickly but with a little less urgency. Maybe, just maybe, he was starting to trust that Chris wasn't going to take the food away and that he didn't want anything from him. Though he was pretty certain Pavle was still looking for an angle of some sort in all this.

"We work some more?" Pavle asked, standing in the back sitting room, staring out the windows.

"You can go outside if you want. Please stay in the yard, but you can go out there any time you want." Chris wasn't sure how that sounded to Pavle. He didn't want him leaving the yard for his own safety, not because he wanted to hold him prisoner.

"I can?"

"Yes. Have fun."

"We plant more flowers?" Pavle asked.

"I don't have any more now, but I can buy some flowers tomorrow and we can plant them." Chris made a note to pick up a couple flats of annuals that he and Pavle could plant. If Pavle wanted to be outside and garden, Chris wasn't going to tell him no. Hell, he'd let Pavle pick out the flowers he wanted. Who knew what he'd end up with, but it didn't matter. Outside flowers went with everything. They were bright pops of color that the yard could use all summer long.

He took Pavle's new clothes up to his room, and then joined him out in the yard.

Outside, the air was fresh with a slight chill, because of an amazing breeze. Chris brought Pavle a sweatshirt, and they sat quietly in the yard.

Chris's phone rang and he answered it. "Deputy Anducci."

"Chris, it's Briggs." His voice rang with concern. "Is Mr. Kasun safe at the moment?" It was a strange way of referring to the situation without mentioning their location, but Chris went with it.

"Yes. Why?" Chris felt a chill race up his back, but he had to keep his voice normal because Pavle was already watching him like a hawk. A second call came in from Marie. He declined it and would call her back.

"I'm just checking," Briggs said. "There has been an incident at one of the safe houses in town. One of my witnesses is there, and I wanted to make sure your assignment wasn't jeopardized."

"No. He's safe," Chris reported.

"Okay. I will let you know when I know more."

He disconnected as another call from Marie came in. "This is Chris."

"Oh, thank God I caught you." He'd thought Marie immune to drama, but apparently something had gotten to her. "The safe house where we picked up Pavle yesterday has burned to the ground."

"What?"

"Yes. They left five gallons of gasoline outside, so when it went up, it blew the building off its foundation before engulfing it in a fireball. The other residents got out, except for one who was blown out into the yard. She's in emergency now. I need to check on her and everyone else, but I thought you should know." Marie seemed to take the welfare of those in her care very seriously. Chris liked her even more, if that was possible.

"Okay. Thank you." He got up and slowly went into the house to leave Pavle in peace. "Have the police said anything about motive or who might have done this?"

"Not yet. But it was right outside Pavle's room, and…."

He kept calm, his training kicking in. "We can't jump to any conclusions. Granted, it is suspicious that this happened the day after we took him out. How long had he been there?"

"Three days. They're working quickly now. The first safe house had people watching it and we had to move everyone. The second was threatened within a few days of Pavle arriving, and now this. I know it's not definitive, but let's not let common sense take a breather either. I know in my heart that someone is after him, but I'm not sure why exactly. I don't have access to what he's told the police so far, but he has told me what happened to him."

"I need to get a look at his statement," Chris said. "There has to be something. If he's been left alone for years but now that he's in protective custody, he's got someone scared, then there's something locked inside his head that they're afraid he's going to tell." His mind spun as he thought of possibilities. "Or he's already told the police something and they've found out." Either option meant there was someone inside the department who was dirtier than a pig in slop. Pun intended. Access to that information was heavily restricted, and even the database was coded so that very few people had access to all the information. It would be easy to verify and discount them.

"Okay. I wanted to let you know." She huffed out a shaky breath, definitely rattled.

He shook his head even though there was no one to see it. "What do you think I should tell Pavle? Part of me thinks he deserves to know what is happening, and another screams to protect him from all this. But if I do, am I being like the people who held him?"

Marie grew more serious. "You, Deputy Chris, are nothing at all like the man who held him. That kind of man would never think of him in any way. He is narcissistic to the extreme, and everything is about him. No doubt about that. It's all about what he wants and has nothing to do with Pavle or his welfare. He was property, pure and simple." She paused. "My advice is to think about it. You'll know what to do. But my general rule is that secrets suck."

"I'll keep that in mind."

She ended the call, saying that she had another coming in.

Chris hung up, then watched Pavle sitting in the garden for a bit. He really didn't know what to do, and he didn't want Pavle to feel trapped, but this was real. Even if Pavle wasn't the reason for setting the safe house on fire, there was that chance, and that meant Chris needed to be extra vigilant.

He returned outside, the cooler evening air coming in as the wind began to change. "Do you want to help me make dinner?" Chris asked. Pavle could sit out here as long as he wanted, but Chris hoped he was willing to join him.

"Okay." Pavle stood and reluctantly came inside.

Chris locked all the doors for the night and then got out the things for dinner. "Have you ever had scalloped potatoes?" he asked, and Pavle looked at him like he was speaking Greek. "Can you make salad?"

Pavle nodded, and Chris set him up with the makings and a bowl, letting Pavle tear some lettuce while he thinly sliced the potatoes and cut up the ham. Then he made the light cream sauce and handed Pavle a knife to cut the tomatoes.

Pavle looked at it and then at him, and Chris knew something had clicked inside him. It was like the light went on in his eyes and some additional part of him believed what Chris and Marie had been telling him. Chris had just given him a weapon, something none of his captors would have ever done.

"I cut tomato."

"Yes. Just be careful." Chris watched as Pavle cut up the tomato with the same precision he did everything else. A cucumber was next, then radishes.

Chris put the casserole dish in the oven and helped Pavle finish the salad with some shredded cheese. "In case you were hungry, I thought we could eat the salad now and have the rest when it's done." Chris had figured out that Pavle was always hungry.

"We watch TV?"

Chris nodded, got out the salad dressings, and let Pavle taste them before choosing which one he wanted. Then he portioned the salads out, dressed them, and they went into the living room to sit on the sofa. Chris brought them each some water and turned on the television. "Did you ever get to watch television… before?"

"Sometimes. But mostly when they not see me. I watch television through the window sometimes." Pavle took a big bite and hummed. "This good." He ate some more and continued making yummy sounds. "I no get... these." He pointed to the lettuce, and Chris figured he meant fresh things. "Is real good." He finished his salad, and Chris took care of the dishes.

They watched a rerun of *The Nanny* until the potatoes were ready. Pavle obviously didn't get much of the humor, but he laughed when Chris laughed and relaxed back into the cushions, sitting not nearly as rigidly as he had the day before. Chris decided to sleep on what he wanted to tell him about the safe house. Tomorrow morning was going to be soon enough to relate difficult news.

# CHAPTER 3

CHRIS WOKE in the middle of the night to the sound of someone downstairs, moving around. He hoped to hell it was Pavle, but got up, silently slipping into his robe. A crash had him grabbing his gun from the table beside the bed, and he left his room, heading right for the stairs. He descended as quietly as he could, listening for any other sound but hearing nothing at all. He made it to the bottom of the steps and paused.

Slowly, step by step, room by room, he cleared the front of the house, making his way through the kitchen to the back sitting room, gun at the ready. He flipped on the light. Pavle squeaked, and Chris relaxed, lowering the gun and breathing a sigh of relief.

On the floor, pieces of the glass dish Chris kept on the table next to the chair glittered in the incandescent light. Pavle was curled up in the chair, legs to his chest. He shook like a branch in a tornado. Clearly Pavle expected punishment, hurt, pain. It was written in the way he hid every tender area of his body.

"It's okay," Chris said as gently as he could, his heart finally quieting in his ears. "Don't move." He hurried out, slipped his feet into an old pair of gardening shoes he kept by the back door, then grabbed the broom to sweep up the glass. Pavle was barefoot, so Chris needed to get the mess cleaned. Then, once he'd dumped the shards in the trash can, he returned to a still-cowering Pavle. "I mean it, it's okay. It was just a dish I keep nuts and stuff in." He touched Pavle's arm to get his attention, keeping it light and gentle, meaning to soothe him. He hadn't expected the surge of anger at the people who'd held Pavle that raced through him. "I'm not going to hurt you."

Pavle stayed still, probably thinking this was some sort of trap.

Chris turned on the table lamp and flipped off the brighter overhead light. Then he sat in the other chair, waiting him out. Pavle had to come to his own conclusions.

Pavle slowly unwound himself from the tiny ball he'd pulled himself into. "You no hurt? Not mad?"

"No. I won't do that to you." Chris didn't move, letting Pavle slip out of the darkness that seemed to nearly overwhelm him. "What are you doing down here?"

"I no sleep. Want to see outside," Pavle answered softly. "Never get to see outside for long times."

"I know. And you can go outside and look outside all you want. But it's the middle of the night and you need to try to sleep. Are you thirsty?" Chris asked.

"Juice?"

Chris nodded and stood, letting Pavle come with him to the kitchen, where he got a small glass and poured some grape juice for Pavle. He rinsed it out when Pavle was done and turned out the lights, heading back upstairs. Pavle went to his own room and Chris to his, but after a few minutes he left again, pretending to go to the bathroom, but really making sure Pavle was settled. Then he washed up quickly and got back in bed.


"ARE YOU sure?" Chris asked the following morning when he called in to the station to talk to Briggs, who was working with the Carlisle Police on the fire.

"Yes. If they'd just wanted to burn the house down, they could have been less exposed and have had a better chance simply by going into the garage or around to the other side of the house. They purposely put the accelerant outside that room and that window. It was deliberate and targeted."

That was not the kind of news Chris was hoping for first thing in the morning. He sipped his coffee. "Okay." He sighed. "I was hoping that...."

"I know what you were hoping, and I was too. There could be a lot of reasons why someone might do this, but my gut is telling me they were after your charge. Keep him safe."

"Why are they so acutely interested now, at this moment?"

Briggs didn't answer at first, and Chris waited. "I'll call you back in a minute, dear." Then the line went dead, and Chris wondered what the fuck was going on. He refilled his mug, glad Pavle was still sleeping. His phone rang as he was just finishing his second cup of the coffee. "Sorry. We had ears. I'm outside on break. Look, I talked to Red at Carlisle PD. He told me, officer to officer, that Pavle is a gold mine. They think he can describe, in detail, each person who has owned or handled him. Including the men who trafficked him into the Super Bowl. So it's a real chance to nail some of these guys."

"How do they know this?"

"They found an interpreter of sorts, apparently." Briggs didn't sound too enthusiastic. "Red said that they had a hard time and isn't sure how effective they are going to be. I wish one of us spoke his language. That would be ideal, but we work with the tools we have."

"I'll do whatever I can to keep him safe. Let me know what you find out." Chris ended the call as Pavle shuffled into the room, still in his pajamas and bleary-eyed. Chris poured and handed him a mug of coffee.

"Thank you." Pavle smelled it, a smile curling his lips. "I miss this for a long time." He sniffed and turned away. Chris wanted to comfort him—God, that was something he felt a million times a day, it seemed.

His phone rang again and Chris snatched it up. "Yes?"

"Is that how you talk to your nanna?" The gentle snap in her voice was hard to mistake.

"Sorry," Chris groaned. "It's been a busy morning."

"You must be busy. I was starting to think you were dead in one of those raids, like I see on television. You don't call or visit, and I sit here wondering." His grandmother was a hoot. And shit on a shingle, he should have thought of her before. He really was getting too much into his own head. "I called the office and they said you were off, so I want you to come to lunch. I make ćevapi."

"Nanna, I have someone staying with me…." He glanced at Pavle and then away once again, having a sudden lightbulb moment. "How much do you remember about the old country?"

"Like it was yesterday," she answered. Nanna had emigrated with his grandfather, escaping communist Yugoslavia. "Why?"

"I think I will come to lunch, and I'm going to bring a friend." She was just the break he needed. "I'll call before we leave, okay? What do you want me to bring?"

"Yes." She sounded delighted. "Just come. I want to see you, and this young man of yours." His grandmother seemed to have the wrong idea, but he wasn't worried about that. She'd get the picture soon enough. "Come at eleven, and we'll have a spot of tea before lunch." She hung up before Chris could argue.

He stared at the blank screen on his phone and set it down. "Pavle, would you like to visit my grandmother? She invited us for lunch," Chris asked, unsure what sort of reception the idea was going to get.

"She know…." Pavle pointed to himself, color blazing on his cheeks. "Ummm… about what do?" He stood and leaned over the chair, butt out.

Chris got the idea. "No." He closed his eyes, because he should absolutely not be noticing how those pajamas tightened over Pavle's backside. "That is something for you to share… not me. People have no right to know unless you want them to."

Pavle shook his head. "No one know. I shame."

"No. You are not shamed. You did what you had to in order to live. You are strong." Chris made a muscle with his arm, pointing at Pavle. "You… strong."

Pavle turned back to him and shook his head. "I do this to me."

"No. *They* did this to you. You survived." Chris wondered how he could make Pavle understand, but realized he wasn't going to, not easily. Pavle's feelings and convictions had been born of years of captivity, and they weren't going to be undone in a single conversation.

"I not tell anyone."

"That's up to you." Chris patted the chair lightly, and Pavle sat down. Chris slid his coffee closer and let the topic fall away. "No one is going to push you. Do you understand?" God, the distress in Pavle's eyes burned like lava.

"I cannot. It is shame. I bring shame." Pavle lowered his gaze. "What I did bad. I bad. I…." His shoulders bounced and Pavle's breath heaved. He jumped to his feet and raced through the house to a corner in the living room, where he hid his face behind his hands. Chris could see him through the doorways, standing alone and scared, and there was fuck all he could do about it. Many times in his relatively short career he had experienced frustration over things he couldn't help, but this was the very worst.

Chris pushed his mug aside and traced Pavle's path through the house. "You are not bad. You are strong." Maybe if he heard it often enough, instead of the messages that had been fed to him for so many months, something would penetrate.

"I shame," Pavle mumbled, his face covered.

Chris could hold back no more. He stepped forward and touched Pavle's shoulder. "You are good," he whispered. "And there is no shame." Certainly not as far as he was concerned. Pavle was a victim. "You don't have to tell anyone."

Pavle shook, and Chris guided him to a chair. He needed a chance to breathe and calm down, to compose himself. At least that's what Chris hoped. Maybe he should call Marie, but he didn't want to leave Pavle alone long enough to do that.

"I shame."

"Did you choose to do what you did? Did you have a choice?" Chris asked quietly.

"I no choosed, but I still shame," Pavle said softly. Of course he would be ashamed of what happened to him; that made sense to Chris. But Pavle acknowledging that he didn't choose it was a step in the right direction.

"Do you want to go upstairs, take a shower, and get dressed?" Chris purposely phrased it that way in order to help Pavle remember what he needed to do and give him a way out of this situation. He understood Pavle was lost and trying to find his way in a world he didn't know and couldn't understand most of the time. "You don't have to go with me, but Nanna is making ćevapi."

A light went on behind Pavle's eyes. "She know Serbia?" He sniffed and wiped his eyes.

"Nanna is Serbian. Come with me, and she will cook for us."

Pavle thought for a few seconds and nodded. Then he left the room and slowly climbed the stairs as though each foot weighed a ton. A war had to be raging inside him—his shame versus any reminder of the home he was taken from. Chris hoped the reminder would win out.

Chris decided to make breakfast to give Pavle some time on his own. Normally he was the kind of guy who grabbed something on the way to work, but he thought Pavle would respond to food. Chris needed to make sure Pavle learned he didn't need to worry about his next meal or that food was going to be used as a control measure.

Bacon and pancakes drew Pavle into the kitchen like nectar to a honeybee, and Chris set a plate in front of him, along with some juice.

"You not mad?"

"That you argued with me? No." Chris brought his own plate to the table and sat down. "You are allowed to have your own opinion and feelings." He lightly touched Pavle's hand, surprised at how soft it was. "You can think the way you want. That's part of how things should work. The only way you are going to make me mad is if you hurt me... or yourself."

Pavle's eyes grew wide and then he nodded. "Go outside?"

"I wish we could, but it's raining." Damn it all, he had forgotten to get more plants. "But we can stop and get some flowers on the way to Nanna's, and once it stops, we can plant them. Is that okay? Lots of pretty flowers, and you can choose." Chris ate his pancakes, which were nothing like his mother's, but good nonetheless.

"Do you go work?" Pavle asked.

"On Friday, so I have one more day out of the office." Chris wasn't sure what he was going to do with Pavle once he had to return. He didn't like the idea of leaving him alone all day without protection, and he couldn't take him into the station. Maybe he'd ask Marie for some advice. Briggs might be able to help as well. He'd need to ask the sheriff's permission to stay with Pavle. God, he hated talking to that man. There was something off about him that made it unsettling. But be that as it may, the sheriff was still his boss and he wanted to keep his job, so he had to make the guy happy.

Pavle finished his rather precise eating, and Chris made a mental list of the things he needed to get done today. Once he finished his breakfast and took care of the dishes, Chris wandered to the back of the house. He stood near the windows as the rain pelted the new leaves and puddled in the garden.

"Is pretty, but wet," Pavle said from next to him. "I want see sun again."

"You will," Chris promised, "but it's going to be rainy and cloudy for a few days." He hated these prolonged days of overcast. Being cooped up in the house wasn't a lot of fun, and Chris wondered what they could do. He didn't want to take Pavle out any more than necessary.

Chris turned away from the windows and opened the closet door. This room had likely been a screened-in porch once, and maybe some sort of garden room before that. Someone enclosed it long ago, but one of the remnants of the past use of the space was the closet, which Chris used for games and things like that.

He pulled out some colored pencils and a couple of drawing tablets. "When I was a kid, I used to draw flower pictures for my mom. Maybe we could draw now if you'd like." Chris set everything on the small table in the corner and got a couple of chairs. They could look out into the wet spring garden, and he figured maybe Pavle could dream of his sunshine. If nothing else it would pass the time for a few hours.

Chris passed a pad and the pencils to Pavle, then sat down.

"I… make picture?" Pavle asked.

Chris nodded. "Of whatever you want." He took the green pencil and began outlining leaves and stems. Chris had been pretty good at this back in the day, and his mom had loved the pictures. He thought of getting an umbrella and picking a few flowers to bring inside so they could look at them closely.

Pavle stared at the paper and pencils, his cheeks draining of color. Chris was wondering what he'd done wrong when Pavle slowly lifted one of the tablets and picked up the black pencil. "This for me?"

"Yes. You can have it." Chris indicated the tablet, and Pavle smiled, holding it to him the way he had the jeans. After a few seconds, he opened it, scooted his chair back, and began to draw.

Chris swallowed and excused himself, going to the kitchen where he could breathe. How in the hell could Pavle have been so mistreated and hurt that paper, something Chris had had in abundance all his life, was like a gift from heaven? How could someone treat another human being that way? Chris's stomach did a flip-flop. He hurried to the bathroom, but thankfully he didn't get sick, though he wanted to. Instead, he got angry. No matter what, he was going to find those people and string them up by their nuts.

He pulled out his phone and sent a message to Marie, who called him right back.

"What's happened?" she asked breathlessly.

"Nothing new." Chris explained about the tablet. "I needed to speak with someone, and you were the one person I thought about." He paced the kitchen. "I want to kick them into the middle of next week." He shook his fist at nothing, just because he was so angry. "What do I do?"

"Turn that anger into action. Keep Pavle safe so he can testify." The rustling of papers reached through the phone. "The FBI wants to speak with Pavle next week. I'll be there with him just to make sure they don't try to push him too hard." She sighed into the phone. "Just take care of him and look after him."

"I'll do my best. But what should I do once I have to go back to work?" Chris asked, and Marie growled.

"I hate your new boss. Just saying. Check with the department, but when we requested you, we did so with the understanding that this was your work assignment.

I'll make a few calls to verify it, and they should be in contact. Let me know if they aren't, and I'll rattle some cages."

He agreed, thanked her for her help, and ended the call. Chris felt a little better. Marie was right. He needed to channel his anger into something constructive.

Chris got a couple of glasses of water and brought them into the back room. Pavle had his head lowered, working on his drawing diligently, tongue between his teeth. Chris set down the glassed and took his seat once again before returning to his own flower picture.

Time ticked by, and Chris checked the clock on the cable box. "Nanna is expecting us in a little while. Do you want to have lunch with her?"

"Yes. I meet her," Pavle said, closing the tablet, then patting it gently with a sigh. Chris didn't ask to see what he'd been working on. When Pavle was ready to show him, he hoped he would.

He went to the closet and got jackets for both of them. Pavle practically swam in the one Chris lent him, but Chris wanted to make sure he was warm and dry on this chilly spring morning. Chris checked the locks in front and led them out of the back door, to the garage and the car.

The nursery was on the way to Nanna's, so he stopped and led Pavle inside.

Pavle took one look at the rows and rows of color in bloom and gasped, clutching his hands together. "I never see so much pretty before."

"You can pick any kind you like," Chris said, indicating the area for Pavle to choose from.

Pavle went up and down each row, looking at the flowers, sniffing and gently touching. He was intensely gentle, almost caressing the flowers as he went.

"These," he said, pointing to the large orange and yellow marigolds. "These and these." He picked out purple and pink petunias, and Chris got half a flat of each color and took them to the register. Pavle practically skipped along in front of him.

Once he paid for the plants and got them loaded into the trunk, they continued on to Nanna's. She'd lived in the same house for fifty-plus years. The small Victorian home, with its white gingerbread porch, was like something out of a storybook. Chris had always thought of the place as a fairy-tale house.

"It's about time," Nanna said as he opened the door. She unlocked the one on the inside, clearly waiting for them. "Terrible day, but I have munchies all set."

"This is Pavle," Chris introduced.

"It nice meet you." Pavle gave her a little bow.

"Nanna, Pavle is Serbian," Chris explained.

Her eyes widened, and when she spoke to him, Pavle's eyes lit up. He followed her inside, and Nanna led him to the sofa, where they both sat. Questions and answers—Chris had little idea what they were speaking about, but Pavle talked for a long time, his hands waving as he got more and more excited and animated.

Nanna patted his hand, and after a while, she stood, finally turning to Chris. "He is a good boy," she pronounced. "I need to make lunch, but I won't be long." She then spoke with Pavle once more, smiling at him. "You stay here with him."

"I will." Chris watched as Pavle's gaze followed Nanna until she disappeared.

"She very good lady," Pavle said before eyeing the cookies and tea on the table.

Chris handed him the plate and cup, and Pavle ate a cookie, and then a second.

The scent of rich spices and sausage drifted in from the kitchen—the scent of his childhood, bringing back days when he used to stay with Nanna, playing on this living room floor while she cooked. He wondered what sort of memories this conjured up for Pavle. He hoped they were good ones from before his life had changed so dramatically.

"Boys, come into the kitchen," she called, and Chris guided Pavle inside.

"Like Mama," Pavle whispered as tears ran down his cheeks.

Nanna hurried over, talking to him softly and then hugging him closely, whispering comfort. Chris didn't have to speak the language to know that tone. She was the comforter-in-chief of the family, be that with food, hugs, or understanding. That was his nanna. A hundred pounds of love all wrapped in a gray-haired, petite, sometimes snappy and demanding package that he wouldn't trade for the world.

"Sit," she said, and brought Pavle a plate with sausages, tomatoes, and some onions.

Pavle stared at it, still crying as he took the first bite. "Is so good…." He gulped and ate a few more bites. Once again, Pavle had taken Chris by complete surprise. He should have anticipated the intense reaction to Nanna's food and the way he almost seemed overwhelmed by it.

She spoke to him softly, and Pavle reached out to hold her hand. Chris's body actually tingled as the skin around Pavle's eyes smoothed out and his mouth lost some of its rigidity. He was relaxing, but not like he was putting his feet up. Instead, it seemed like Nanna was the first person he'd met in four years who truly understood him.

"Nanna," Chris said as he ate. "There are some things I need to talk over with Pavle, but I think it would be best if you were with us to help make sure he understands."

She nodded. "You know I'll help any way I can." She gestured to Pavle. "There are things he doesn't want to talk about."

"I know, and I promised I wouldn't force him." Chris nodded to Pavle. "You can tell Nanna whatever you want. It's okay. She will understand."

"Pavle," Nanna said as she finally brought over her own plate. She always served herself last, and sometimes Chris wondered if she ever got a hot meal. Once she sat, she turned to Pavle and began to talk. Chris wished he understood what she was saying. Pavle listened with rapt attention, even putting his hand over his mouth at one point. Then he nodded slowly and took her hand, comforting her.

"What are you talking about?" Chris asked once their conversation seemed to have come to a break.

"I told him about how Vladimir and I left Yugoslavia. I told him what happened to me and how we got out. We were children and stupid, too young to know better, but we knew we wanted out. I told him what happened to me and what I did in order to make sure we could be free."

"What don't I know?"

"That I traded my virtue for our freedom. Vladimir and I were about to be caught. So I gave myself up. The guard who found us was a sloppy and lazy man. I pretended that I liked him and ensured his attention was elsewhere so Vladimir could cross the border. Then, when his pants were down and he was vulnerable, I knocked him out and hurried to join Vladimir. He and I crossed the rough terrain through Macedonia and into Greece. From there we made it to the US, as you know." She looked back at Pavle as Chris digested this little bit of new information, completely aghast at what she had been through.

"Did the guard know you were pregnant?" Chris asked.

She turned back to him. "No. We didn't exactly talk about our lives. It was fast, and I did what I had to do. Vladimir was unhappy with me, but he and I were out and had the chance at a better life. That was all that mattered." She paused. "I did what I had to do, and Vladimir knew that."

Chris blinked and wanted to kill the man who had hurt his nanna. He'd always known she was strong, but the steel in her spine blew him away. Chris went back to his lunch, still digesting what his grandmother had told him. When he was done, he carried his plate to the sink, nearly dropping it in his preoccupation. Pavle had finished as well, and Chris took care of his dishes, feeling a bit like an outsider as they talked.

"Chris, I'm going to need the air conditioner in a few weeks. Could you get the cover off it and make sure everything is working right?" She smiled, and he knew he was being dismissed. They needed to talk, and that was part of why he'd brought Pavle over here.

Thankfully the rain had let up. He grabbed an umbrella from where Nanna kept them by the back door, then went out in the drippy afternoon. He wasn't in a hurry, so he took care of the air conditioner cover and put it in the garage. Then he picked up sticks in the yard and swept off her covered outdoor patio before returning inside. He checked that the air-conditioning was working and that it blew cool air before shutting the system down again.

Pavle and Nanna talked nonstop and showed no signs of slowing down, with Pavle doing a lot of the speaking. Chris tried to cut in a few times, but failed and waited for Nanna.

"Chris, sweetheart," Nanna said eventually. "What is it that you want to talk to Pavle about?"

The two of them sat together on her sofa, and Chris took the nearby chair, leaning forward. "Can you translate for me? This needs to be clear, and please don't ask any questions of your own. It's important that I know he understands what happened and why it's happening. Okay?"

"Of course." She rolled her eyes, but Chris knew his nanna.

"Yesterday, the safe house that Pavle was staying at had a fire," he said, then waited for her to explain. "One of the women is in the hospital and is being cared for. The others are fine."

She talked briefly with Pavle. "Which one is hurt?" Nanna asked, falling into the role of translator pretty well.

"I don't know her name, but Marie will be able to answer the questions when she visits, if she's allowed. Marie is the social worker who has been working with Pavle." He waited while Nanna spoke. "The thing is, the fire was not an accident. It was set deliberately, and they were targeting Pavle." He figured the direct approach was best, watching Pavle closely as she conveyed what he'd said.

Pavle blinked and sat very still. "I hurt her. It… me. I do this."

"No. You didn't do this." He turned to Nanna. "Please tell him that this is not his fault. We are working to find out who is leaking information and shouldn't be. It's not his fault at all."

Nanna nodded and smiled quickly before relaying the message, shaking her head and then taking Pavle's hands in hers before talking once again.

"It's not your fault," Chris repeated.

"Pavle says he knows that, but he feels like it is. All this is happening because of him. I told him it was because of the men who are doing this. He is not responsible for them." She seemed as concerned as Chris was. "He has been gaslighted. I saw that movie you know, very disturbing."

It was shocking that she knew what that was. "Yeah, he has."

"Then this guilt is going to take some time for him to deal with." She continued holding Pavle's hand. "You are a good boy, you know, and Serbian grandmothers don't lie." She smiled at Pavle, and thankfully he smiled back. "You are welcome here any time." She squeezed Pavle's hand. "Come visit whenever you want to."

And at that moment, as if to prove the weatherman wrong, the skies lightened up and the sun did its best to try to shine through the window.

"Can we plant flowers?" Pavle asked, turning to look out the window.

"Young man, I'm sure my grandson will let you do whatever you want." She winked at him, and Chris groaned softly. Damn it all, Nanna was matchmaking. It ran in the family, or at least Nanna said it did, and she was working what she thought was her mojo.

"Why don't we wait for it to dry out a little so we don't end up with mud up to our ears? And Nanna, please be good." He flashed her a mock glare. He had never been able to stay angry with her for more than a few seconds.

"She good," Pavle said.

"He's teasing me," Nanna told him with a gentle smile. "Chris is always nice to his nanna." There was an "or else" gleam in her eye that Chris couldn't argue with. "Now, I have cookies and some tea for dessert." She stood and got steady on her feet before heading to the kitchen.

"Are you okay?" Chris asked Pavle.

"Yes. I okay. Nanna is nice. She remind me of my nanna." A dark sadness washed across his face. "She died before I came here."

Chris shifted to sit next to Pavle. "Then you can think of my nanna as your nanna." He patted him on the shoulder. "How much did you tell her?"

Pavle swallowed. "All. She understand."

"Yes. Nanna understands a lot, and not many things surprise her. I'm glad you could talk to her." Chris turned so he was facing Pavle, and as he watched, Pavle crumpled in front of him, throwing his arms around Chris's waist, burying his face in his shoulder, the tears coming hard. Chris held him, trying his best to keep the wetness out of his own eyes and failing.

Nanna briefly appeared in the doorway carrying a tray and turned back, leaving the two of them alone.

"It's okay. You're allowed to feel bad. You were used," Chris said. Pavle had part of his life ripped away from him, and now he was trying to put his life back together, only Chris figured he had no idea what the finished puzzle was going to look like, so none of the pieces seemed to fit.

"They took me. They lied." The tears continued to fall. "They took my everything… my papers…."

"I know. Marie is working to see if she can find them." Chris was well aware that the chances of anyone finding Pavle's original passport and documents were pretty slim. Still, once they found the man who'd been holding him, they could get lucky. Chris sure hoped so.

Nanna came in, and Pavle jumped back, wiping his face. He slunk back on the sofa, like he wanted to disappear. "I sorry."

"Pish," Nanna said, and set down the tray, talking to Pavle, who let go of some of his tension.

"There are some questions I need answers to. Do you think you can help me?" Chris asked.

"Yes. But not today." She handed Pavle a cup and then passed one to Chris before taking her teacup. She sat slowly and sipped, pinkie out as was proper.

"Then come to lunch tomorrow," Chris offered. She was probably right. Pavle needed a chance to digest everything that had happened.

They ate cookies, and Pavle sat silently. Chris could almost feel him pulling away again.

"Go ahead and take him home. He's been through a lot. I'll come over for lunch, and maybe you could see if this Marie person could join us. We have a lot to talk about." She extended her hand, and Pavle reached out to her. "I'll see you tomorrow." She switched to Serbian for a bit.

Chris finished his tea and took the dishes to the kitchen. Then he said goodbye and kissed her on the cheek. "Do you want me to pick you up?"

"No, I can drive." That was about the scariest thing Chris had heard in the last few days. Just the thought of Nanna on the road was enough to send a wave of cold fear racing up his spine for every single other driver. "Don't start with me or you'll be on my shit list, right alongside your mother. I'm a perfectly capable driver, and she knows it." She glared at the phone for a second as though it had offended her. "I'll come to your house and see what you have to eat." In other words, she was going to take over his kitchen and make enough food to feed both him and Pavle for a month.

God, he loved his nanna.

Chris headed for the door, and Pavle said goodbye to Nanna. She hugged him and kissed him on the cheek before hugging him again. Pavle returned her embrace, and a stab of jealousy shot to Chris's gut. He knew he was being stupid, but he wanted to be the one Pavle was holding that way. "You are good," she stage-whispered, releasing Pavle. Then she saw them to the door, and Chris motioned for Pavle to go in front of him as they headed to the car. He'd hoped Nanna would be able to break through Pavle's shell. He hadn't expected her to do it so well.

"I like her. She…." Pavle seemed to search for the word. "Special."

Yeah, that was his nanna in a word.

# CHAPTER 4

"WHAT DO you do all day?" Briggs asked during Chris's daily call to the station. Once Briggs had informed him that guarding Pavle was his assignment, he called in at least daily and had been able to stop worrying over how to look after Pavle when he was on shift. Over the past five days, Chris had been able to avoid talking to the sheriff directly and went through Briggs. "It has to be boring as heck sitting around there with nothing to do."

The sarcasm wasn't lost on Chris. He glanced to where Pavle sat at the table in the back room, drawing and looking out the window. He'd spent a lot of time with that sketch pad and those pencils, but so far he hadn't shown Chris or anyone else what he was doing.

"We garden and watch television. Pavle isn't a prisoner, so we go to the store, but limit our time away in case he's spotted."

"Good. We've had indications that there are people looking for him. At least that's the word on the street." Though Briggs usually called from outside the station so they could talk freely, he spoke quietly. "But I'm a little concerned. My gut is telling me that someone is feeding them information. If it's within the sheriff's

carefully and clearly to be helpful. He also suspected
that television helped… or hurt, as the case might be.

"Yes. And after they are done, you and I will have
lunch. Do you want to eat at a restaurant?"

"McDonalds. Like on TV?" Pavle asked with a grin.

It wasn't Chris's favorite place, but if Pavle wanted to try, that was fine with him. "I can go through the
drive-through and we can eat back here." It was safer,
with less chance of them being seen. Chris didn't want
to deny Pavle one of the few things he'd asked for.

"Okay." Pavle returned his attention to his drawing
and then closed the sketch pad and held it to himself
as he stood and went outside to sit in the sun. Chris
watched him through the window as Pavle turned his
face upward.

Briggs was right; he needed to remember that Pavle was a charge under his protection, a professional relationship, and he wasn't supposed to develop feelings
for him. But, fucking hell, it was too late and Chris already knew it. He'd take a bullet for Pavle without a
second thought. God, he was so screwed.

Chris went upstairs and showered. He dressed ca-
sually so he wouldn't draw attention to himself or Pavle, then got Pavle.

"What will they ask?" Concern filled Pavle's eyes,
and his posture was rigid after he came back inside.

"Probably much of the same things that the Carlisle Police did. Just be truthful as you can. That's all
anyone expects of you."

Pavle nodded. "You be there?"

"If that's what you want. I will try." Chris wasn't
sure if he would be allowed to be in the room, but he
intended to press for it. Pavle needed someone there
who was on his side and looking out for him. Of course,

Marie would be there as well, but he didn't know if they'd allow her to stay either. "Are you ready to go?"

Pavle nodded. "They help me?" he asked more softly this time.

Chris would have loved to say yes, these people would help him, but the truth was they had their own agenda. The FBI were great law enforcement officers, but their perspective could be one-sided, and that wasn't necessarily going to be the best one for Pavle. "They are good people. But I will always help you if I can."

Pavle walked toward the door. "I know you help me." He continued looking outside. "You are nice to me, and I like you for that."

Chris had no idea what to say. He decided to go for what he thought was safe. "I like you too."

Pavle locked his gaze on Chris's, and Chris couldn't move, mesmerized by the flash of innocence in Pavle's eyes. On the surface it seemed ridiculous to think of Pavle as innocent after what he'd been through, but he was in some ways, and Pavle deserved to keep that for as long as possible.

"We go now?" Pavle asked.

Chris nodded and handed him the jacket he now thought of as Pavle's. They headed out to the car, and Chris drove them to the courthouse. They went in the back entrance, through security, and up to one of the conference rooms.

Marie stood outside the door and greeted Pavle and Chris as a man stepped into the hall.

"I'm Special Agent Griffith." He shook hands with all three of them.

"Deputy Chris Anducci. And this is Marie Foster and Pavle Kasun," Chris said as they shook hands.

"Please come in." Agent Griffith opened the door and revealed another agent standing in the corner. "This is Agent Butler. She will be taking notes for us and she speaks Serbian, so she will be able to translate should the need arise." He motioned to the table and waited for Pavle to sit, then let Marie take the chair next to Pavle. Chris sat against the wall next to Agent Butler.

Agent Butler made a brief introduction in Serbian.

"Mr. Kasun, we're here to discover what happened to you and try to catch the people who did this to you."

"Chris tell me." Pavle leaned forward, placing his pad on the table.

"What is that?" Agent Griffith asked.

"Pavle likes to draw, and I gave him the tablet," Chris said for context. "He wanted to bring it with him, and I didn't think it would do any harm."

"I bring because is important." Pavle opened the cover. The portrait of a man stared out from the paper. "This is man who brought me here." He turned to Chris. "In New-ark." He turned the next page. "This man who sell me." He stared at his own drawing, curling his lip upward. "He mean and hit. Bring me here. Called Pauley." Pavle went through the book, page after page, explaining who each person was and what they had done to him.

Chris had had no idea about the drawings and was spellbound, but more by Pavle than the story he told. Anger and indignation rose inside him to the point that his cheeks heated and he gripped the arm of the chair so tightly, he was actually pulling the wood apart. He was supposed to remain detached and professional, but that was impossible with Pavle and the story he told. He'd known what people went through in this situation— he'd seen case studies—but to hear it in first person made his blood boil.

Agent Griffith was smart enough to let Pavle speak, and only asked questions when he needed more detail or clarification. Chris knew Pavle's drawings were like a gift for Agent Griffith.

"This is man who... use me as slave...," Pavle said as he turned the final page. "He keep me locked in house and...." Pavle didn't have the words, so he switched to Serbian.

The rest of the story was highly graphic, and more than once bile rose in Chris's throat. He wanted to beat the hell out of this worm, but he sat still and quiet, seething with each revelation and detail. The only thing easing the way was that the English words came from Agent Butler rather than Pavle himself, but the toll the ordeal was taking on Pavle showed clearly as his cheeks paled and his eyes hollowed, the light Chris had seen in them the last few days going out completely. Chris flexed his hands, heart racing. The arm of the chair ripped upward, and he held the wood with spindles dangling from it. Embarrassed, he set it on the floor.

"Do you need a few minutes?" Agent Griffith asked. Lord knew Chris did, and Pavle had to need a break. "Agent Butler, would you please get everyone something to drink? I'd like to continue, but a few minutes' pause might be in order."

Pavle stood and closed his notebook, leaving it on the table. "This for you. I no want it," he told Agent Griffith. "I give to you." He passed the book across the table and took a deep breath, then came over to sit in the chair next to Chris. "I good?"

"You were amazing," Chris told him, wondering where Pavle had gotten the strength to describe those acts and how he was treated.

Pavle smiled and leaned against Chris's arm, staying close. Damn, that felt good, and Marie nodded and smiled at him. It seemed she approved.

"Can you go on and answer more questions?" Chris put an arm around him, meaning it for comfort, but Pavle leaned closer, resting against him.

"I answer," he whispered.

"Do you need a few more minutes?" he asked, and Pavle nodded, shaking a little. Not that Chris could blame him for a second.

"I brought him some water," Agent Butler said, coming back into the room.

"Juice?" Pavle asked.

Chris chuckled. "Pavle has developed a real taste for grape or orange juice."

Marie pushed her chair back. "There's some in one of the machines on the upper floor. I'll get some and come right back." Chris noticed that she wiped her eyes as she left the room.

Agent Griffith sat back down, watching them with a slight scowl. "I have to ask what *this* is about." He tilted his head in their direction.

"Deputy Chris is nice to me." Pavle scratched his head. "I need strong, and he strong for me." He sat back up and returned to the table. "You ask questions now."

In those few seconds and with four words, Pavle showed just how strong he truly was, enough for Chris to know that what strength he had paled in comparison. He forced himself to settle down even as he prepared himself to hear the answers to Agent Griffith's questions.

WHAT FELT like hours later, he, Pavle, and Marie left the room.

"That was…." Marie seemed unable to finish her sentence, and all Chris could do was nod.

"I told you I shame," Pavle said, not looking at either of them.

"You are not," Marie argued. "You are strong. You did what you needed to survive. Both FBI people said so. I say so. Chris says so."

If Chris ever needed help, he wanted her on his side. Marie was one tough cookie.

"No shame?" Pavle asked, blinking.

"No. No shame." She gathered him into her arms. "You are not to be ashamed. You are strong, and what you told them will help a lot of people. They will get those men because of you. I know it. And then you will have helped, and…. Regardless, you have no shame."

Pavle nodded and stepped back once Marie released him. They left the courthouse, standing on the sidewalk in the afternoon sun.

"I promised Pavle lunch when we were done, and he asked to go to McDonald's. He likes their commercials."

"I need to get back to my office, but you two have a good lunch." She shook their hands, then headed across the street.

"This way." Chris led Pavle around the side of the building, back to his car, and then headed to lunch. Chris used the drive-through, and since Pavle didn't know what was what, Chris ordered a variety of things for him to try and then headed for home.

He was surprised to see Nanna's old Oldsmobile parked in front of the house. She'd had that car for decades, though nowadays it sat in the garage most of the time. The white car was well on its way to becoming a classic and had just over 20,000 miles on it after all these years.

"Nanna's here," Pavle said with delight, and hurried through the backyard as soon as Chris had closed the overhead door. Chris grabbed the food and followed to find his grandmother in the kitchen, waiting at the table. She *tsk*ed as soon as she saw the bags, and Chris was grateful he'd gotten extra food. So, after setting out plates, they all dug in, with Nanna scarfing down the chicken nuggets. Who would have thought?

Pavle and Nanna chattered, this time somewhat reservedly. Nanna listened and asked questions, at least he assumed so from the inflection. When Nanna hugged Pavle tightly, whispering softly as she rocked him, Chris knew he'd come to the end of the story.

"No guilt, no shame."

Pavle nodded and blinked. "I man now. I be strong."

"You already have been," Chris told him, pushing his plate away. His stomach rebelled as he remembered Pavle's story being related by Agent Butler.

Pavle finished his juice and stood to leave the room, heading toward the bathroom.

"It's okay, sweetheart," Nanna told him once Pavle was gone. "You need to eat and be strong for him. What happened, happened, and you can't change it no matter how much you wish it were possible. But you can help determine how easily Pavle is able to recover. He's going to have to tell this story over and over again, to more police, in court… you know that."

"That's true." And there was little Chris could do about that.

"Then make it as easy on him as possible. That's what you need to do." She leaned closer. "He's pulling some of his strength from you, so you need to be strong. When you react, it falls back on him."

Chris picked up a french fry and dropped it on his plate again. Food just didn't taste good right now. "What do you mean?"

Nanna shook her head. "If you get upset, then he sees that and it makes him upset. He watches you pretty closely and takes his cues from you. Remember that a lot of communication is nonverbal. So be strong." She dunked one of her nuggets in mustard sauce and returned to her lunch. Dammit, she was right, and Chris did need to be strong. There was a lot at stake here, and he had to be there for him. "Now, what happened today?"

Chris gave her a short recap before Pavle returned and sat back down.

"Chris tells me that you can draw," Nanna said, and Pavle nodded. "Do you draw more than people?"

"I draw anything. My mama wanted me to be doctor. I want to be artist." He smiled. "She not happy. But I win and she let me. I draw her pictures." Pavle lowered his gaze to the table, and Chris glanced at Nanna to see if she saw his sadness too.

"When did she die?" Nanna asked.

"Before I come here," Pavle answered. "No one left so I want come here for future. I stupid and believed men, paid them all money have." He sighed. "Now got nothing."

Chris was speechless, and it seemed so was Nanna. She turned away, wiping her eyes with the corner of her napkin. "How did you get away?" Nanna asked.

"Police save me," Pavle said.

Chris shook his head. "Pavle somehow got a note to the neighbors, and they called the police."

Pavle swallowed. "See only little out window. Next house dark all the time, so nothing to see. I all alone for long time. Then lights and people. Little person in room. I see them. They happy. I watch." He chewed on his lower lip. "Master bring food and forget…." He lifted one of the utensils.

"A spoon?" Chris asked.

"Yes. He leave spoon. I rub smaller and turned to open window." He made circular motions, like turning a tool. "I open window and close again." Pavle became excited. "Then it get warm and child window open. I write note and make window open."

It took Chris a few moments to fully understand. "Your window had been screwed shut and you opened it with the spoon?" Pavle had fashioned his own screwdriver to loosen the screws in the window. Chris could imagine him working quickly so he wouldn't be caught.

"Yes. I open window and throw note into house, then close window tight." Pavle made the circular motion again in the opposite direction. "Then I pray. Lots of pray. I ask The Lady to save me." He sighed. "I wait days. Then police come." He shrugged and returned to his lunch.

Everything about Pavle amazed him. After years of being held captive and listening to people tell him that his situation was his own fault, Pavle had the strength and will to try to facilitate his own rescue. That took a hell of a lot of courage.

Pavle moved his chair around to sit next to Chris. "I no want talk anymore," he said softly and leaned against Chris's arm. "Can we be quiet now?"

"Yes. We can be quiet." Chris began to eat slowly, knowing Nanna was watching the two of them together. A smile crept onto her lips as she finished her lunch and slowly stood. She patted Chris's shoulder lightly before heading to the living room.

Chris wound his arm around Pavle's shoulders, cradling him closer. If Pavle wanted comfort, Chris was going to give everything he had, even though he knew he shouldn't be allowing himself to grow this close, and he definitely shouldn't be allowing his heart to get involved. But it seemed it already was whether Chris wanted to allow it or not.

# CHAPTER 5

THE FOLLOWING morning, Chris slowed the car in front of the building where Pavle had been found. He'd left Pavle at home with Nanna so they could talk privately for a little while, which gave him the chance to take a look at the place. After hearing Pavle's story, he needed to see it for himself, and he wasn't going to bring Pavle back here. Chris intended to spare him as much pain as he could.

He parked in the open community space in back and got out at the white two-story house with peeling paint and sagging eaves. It might have been nice once, but it was sad and forlorn now, windows boarded up and police tape flapping in the breeze. Chris walked up and along the side of the house, his gaze sliding upward until a blackened window came into view. He clenched his fists as he realized that was where Pavle had been held. He returned to the front as a Carlisle Police vehicle pulled to a stop behind his car.

"Hey, Red, Carter." He shook both men's hands. "Thanks for doing this."

"No problem," Red said, handing him a pair of gloves. The last thing Chris wanted to do was disturb anything that might be evidence. Red unlocked the door and pushed it open. "The place has been thoroughly gone over." They turned to where Carter sat in the car as backup and then went inside.

Chris crinkled his nose as he stepped inside, the foul, sour air assaulting his senses. "Wow."

"The building has been condemned. Even though it's in the historic district, the borough doesn't think it's salvageable. There's mold all through the walls, and it would be impossible to abate it," Red explained. "The roof has been leaking for a long time, through some of the walls and even weakening the foundation," he added. "We need to be careful of weak spots in the floors."

He led the way to a dismal staircase and up to a dark landing that would have been at home in an old Dracula movie. The door to Pavle's room stood open, and Chris approached it with trepidation—not that he expected to find anything helpful or some ghost waiting there. The room was dark, a sliver of light shining in at the edge of the blackened window.

"Did you find a tool made out of a spoon?" Chris asked. "Pavle used it as a screwdriver to open the window." He stepped inside, and the walls seemed to close in around him. He tried to imagine being kept here for months or years, and the thought, combined with the smell, nearly made him sick.

"Yes," Red answered. "It was in a loose floorboard under where he slept. It's in evidence right now." He paused briefly. "We've left things we didn't take for evidence the way they were. The blankets were folded like that at the foot of the… on the floor." To call what Pavle had slept on a bed was a huge stretch. More like a thin gray pad on bare wood.

Chris went to the window to peer out. He had to see Pavle's view of the world. It was only the house next door. "Let's go." There was nothing else in the otherwise empty room. Not even carpet to cover the scarred, splintering wooden floors.

"Pretty dismal," Red said softly. "How is he doing?"

"Pavle is strong, and he's figuring things out. Taking it day by day, and I think that's the most any of us can ask." Chris left the room and went outside into the morning air, breathing deeply just to cleanse his lungs of the foulness. He looked toward the house next door. "Those must be the people who found Pavle's note." He carefully descended the front stairs and looked up and down the block, trying to get a better feel for the neighborhood. "What do you know about this area?" Chris asked, turning to Red.

"It's a mix. Unfortunately there are too many houses like that one. But there are great people here. Members of the community got together to clean up and build the park a few years ago. There are community garden plots. It's a real local effort." Red stood next to him. "The church has been a big part of that lately."

Chris turned to the left and headed to the front door of the house between the one Pavle had been held in and a small AME church on the other side. He knocked and waited, Red following behind him.

"May I help you?" a black man in dark pants and a shirt with a white collar asked when he opened the door. He was maybe thirty, with bright eyes and a smile. "Has there been trouble?"

"No, Reverend," Red answered. "I was doing some follow-up on the now-empty house next door. Did you or someone here find the note?"

The reverend nodded and opened the door farther. "Please come in." He held the door, and Chris and Red stepped inside the immaculately clean but sparse home, with sturdy furniture that had a lot more function than style. The reverend closed the door and offered them a seat. "I'm Tyrone Watson, and this is my wife, Anika, and my son, Isaac. She found the note."

A gorgeous lady with regal bearing and her hair flowing to her shoulders smiled from the doorway, holding a boy of about two by the hand. "I called the police and reported what I found. Were you able to help whoever threw it?" She turned toward the empty house. "We are all trying to improve this neighborhood and the lives of those in it."

Chris nodded. "We did, and he's being cared for and protected. The man's name is Pavle, and he'd been held for over four years. What you did saved his life and has given him the chance at a future."

"Thank goodness," Reverend Tyrone said softly. "Progress has been slow here, so this is a spot of light for us. Anika and I weren't sure what to make of the note when we first saw it. We had no idea how it got into Isaac's bedroom. The letters were strange, but one word stood out. *Help*. Once we figured out where it came from…." He sighed. "We're glad we could help."

"Pavle understands and speaks some English," Chris explained. "Would you like to meet him? Apparently Pavle used to watch this house through his only view of the world. He said it was dark for a long time, and then he saw you and your son and decided to take a chance. Pavle threw the note, and prayed. You answered his prayers."

Reverend Tyrone clasped his hands together and looked upward. "I think this is the first time we've ever been the answer to someone's prayers." He smiled widely. "If Pavle would like to meet us, we would be honored to meet him."

"Yes, we would." Anika beamed. "Do you know what will happen to the house?"

Red cleared his throat. "It has been condemned and will likely be torn down. It isn't safe, and it's filled with mold. Please warn people to stay away. It is a crime scene and dangerous."

"We will. I'd love nothing more than to have this neighborhood become vibrant again. We're working on a cleanup drive at the moment." The reverend sounded energetic and ready to get to work.

Both Red and Chris smiled. "If we can be of help, be sure to let me know." Red handed the reverend his card. "Stronger communities make everyone safer." Red stood, and Chris followed suit.

"I'll talk to Pavle and pass along your invite to meet. I think he'd like that. You did an amazing thing." Chris shook both Anika's and the reverend's hand, and then they headed to the door. He stepped outside, feeling lighter than he had in days. "Sometimes I love my job...."

Red sighed and nodded. "But sometimes we see so much of the bad that when the good happens, we hardly notice it because we're watching for the next bit of trouble."

"Exactly," Chris agreed. "I hope Pavle will meet with them. I think it could do him some good. He needs to know that there are people who care. But it's his choice."

"Everything go okay?" Carter asked, lowering his window.

"Yeah," Chris answered.

Red stood next to his cruiser, leaning against it. "I think that Pavle has quite a few people who care for him." The knowing look in Red's eye unsettled Chris in a way he didn't expect, as though Red could see into his thoughts. He was supposed to protect Pavle, not perv on him, and while his mind might take him on a journey into fantasy sometimes, he certainly didn't want others to know about it.

"I'm watching out for him, that's all." Fuck it, he should have kept his mouth shut and said nothing. Now Red was going to know exactly where Chris's mind was from his protest. Shit, that was a real rookie mistake and he'd fallen right into it. Rather than trying to explain further, he climbed into his car and lowered the window. "I appreciate all your help. Maybe you and Terry could come over for dinner tonight if you're free. I think it's good that Pavle meet some people in a controlled way so he isn't as shy around everyone."

"Okay. I'll call Terry and make sure he doesn't have anything on the calendar." Red waved as Chris took off, making a call to the station on his way home. Briggs reported that they were no closer to apprehending the man who had held Pavle in town, but apparently the FBI was getting more involved, and the state police wanted to speak with Pavle as well.

"Apparently his ability to draw the people who came in contact with him is of interest to everyone. They want to test his memory abilities, as well as see just how sharp they are."

Chris pulled to a stop at a sign. "What?"

"Yeah. If they're going to prosecute them on the basis of his drawings, then Pavle's memory has to be above reproach. So they want to test him to see how good it really is."

Chris sighed as he went through the intersection. "You have to be kidding me. Pavle isn't someone to push and prod like an animal in a zoo. He's a person. Not a damn guinea pig." He made the turn onto Pomfret and pulled around the back to the garage. "Just being able to draw those images shows he has an amazing memory."

"True, and the FBI has been able to use facial recognition to identify some of the people, particularly his earlier contacts, as low-level mob worker bees. However, one of them has apparently risen through the ranks and has become a bigger fish."

Chris's mouth went dry. That could be the reason for the leaks and the attempts on Pavle's life. The guy who had been a front-line soldier four years ago was now a powerful boss, and he was determined not to get sent up the river for something he'd done years ago. "We'll be careful. But if there is a leak in the department, it isn't going to be too hard for them to figure out that Pavle is staying with me."

"That's why you are officially on family leave and the only one in the department you'll communicate with is me. I don't even want the sheriff to know the details." The contempt rolled off Brigg's tongue. "It's a pain keeping information from him, but it's for your safety, as well as Pavle's. I'm working with Social Services to get Pavle reclassified, and we're leaving a false trail to be followed. We'll see if they pick it up. Meanwhile, stay low and out of sight as much as possible," Briggs said gruffly, but Chris figured that was bravado and part of his demeanor.

"I will. Don't worry." He lowered the garage door and got out, listening before carefully making his way to the house, where he could see Nanna and Pavle moving around the kitchen. "I'll talk to you tomorrow."

"Yeah. I'll call when I'm free to talk, unless there's an emergency." He ended the call, and Chris

continued into the house, which spilled out the entic-
ing scent of Nanna's cooking, onions and spices, strong
and mouthwatering.

"It wasn't necessary to cook," Chris said as he
closed the door, then approached Nanna to kiss her on
the cheek. "But I'm glad you did." His phone vibrated
with a message from Red that he and Terry would be
pleased to join them for dinner. Chris asked Pavle if
that was okay, and Pavle agreed with only slight trepidation. Chris told them six thirty. "Are you staying for
dinner, Nanna?"

"No. I need to go home." She wiped her hands
on a towel before heading to the sink to start on the
mountain of dishes. It seemed she and Pavle had dirtied
almost every pan he had. The dishwasher was already
churning away, and yet there were still a ton to clean.

"It's okay, Nanna. Some friends are coming to dinner. They want to meet Pavle." Chris turned as Pavle
paled in what Chris thought was fear. He immediately
tried to calm him. "They are police like me and really
good. Red is one of the men who found you."

"Oh," Pavle said, relaxing a little, but his posture
remained straight, as though he were on guard.

"I should be going," Nanna said, suddenly in an
all-fired hurry.

Chris walked her to the door and helped her out to
her car, looking up and down the street, the hair on the
back of his neck standing up. He knew he was being
watched, but he couldn't figure out from where. "Be
careful and call me when you get home." He worried
about Nanna driving. She shouldn't be on the road, and
definitely not after dark. His plan had been to get her to
stay for dinner and then spend the night, but she had her
own wishes, and Chris knew better than to push.

"Bah," she said as she slowly bent to get in the car. "Give your nanna a kiss goodbye."

He did as she instructed and watched as she made her way toward home.

Back inside, Chris locked the door and went right to the kitchen to figure out what he was going to serve with what Nanna and Pavle had made. Chris figured Pavle had gone outside the way he normally did, so he started prepping vegetables and pulled steaks out of the freezer, placing them on the thawing tray. Pavle usually liked to help in the kitchen, so when he didn't eventually come in, Chris set his knife down on the cutting board to go look for him.

Pavle wasn't outside and he wasn't in the living room. In a moment of fear, Chris wondered if he had left. He took a deep breath and went upstairs, where he found Pavle in his room, lying on the bed in a fetal position.

"What is it?" he asked as gently as he could. Sometimes he thought he might be starting to understand some of what Pavle was feeling. And then again, there were times when he was completely confused. "There is nothing to be afraid of."

"They will know…," Pavle whispered.

Chris's fingers itched to comfort, but he didn't know if Pavle wanted that. To Chris, comfort meant touch, and there had been times when Pavle had leaned into him. And he had even comforted Pavle on occasion, but he was never really sure if his instincts were right and the comfort would be welcome or if it would turn into a minefield and blow up in his face.

"I know that bothers you, but what did Nanna say?" The two of them seemed to have bonded, at least in some way.

"She say that I good. Not shame." Pavle's voice seemed so childlike in that moment, like his heart was shattering.

"Then believe her... and me. Red is like me. He is a police officer. We see plenty of people who are hurt, and we do not blame them."

"But I shame," Pavle whispered. He kept going back to that, and Chris wondered how he could help him understand that there was no shame in being a victim. That he had been hurt and that people had done things to him and taken away his right to choose... then compounded hurt on top of it by making him think it was all his fault. The entire situation made Chris mad in part because he wanted to be able to fix it. And this probably wasn't something he could fix. Pavle had to work through it on his own. Chris made a mental note to check on Pavle's next therapy appointment.

"I can call and tell them not to come. It will be okay, I promise." Dammit, Chris might have pushed too far.

"No. I come down." Pavle slowly straightened his legs and rolled over, wiping his eyes. "I want to."

Relief washed through Chris. "Do you want to help in the kitchen?" Chris asked, thinking that doing something normal for them would be good. Pavle nodded, and Chris returned downstairs, letting Pavle compose himself.

When Pavle joined Chris in the kitchen, they finished the preparation of dinner together and seasoned the steaks. They had everything ready just as Terry and Red arrived. Chris met them at the door, letting them in and through to the back. Pavle stood behind him, half peering around him.

"Pavle, this is Red. He is a police officer here in Carlisle. And this is his husband, Terry." He kept his voice gentle, hoping they weren't frightening Pavle.

Red slowly extended his hand as Pavle looked at Red and then turned to Chris, tilting his head slightly as though he were trying to make sure he either heard or understood him right. It was a strange moment, and for an instant, Chris thought everything was going to go south at any second. Maybe he'd pushed too far too fast and Pavle's earlier fear around men was going to make an appearance.

"It nice to meet you," Pavle said formally and shyly, shaking their hands because they were offered, looking at Chris most of the time, probably for reassurance, then pulling his hand right back.

"Are you doing well?" Terry asked.

Pavle nodded. "I good." He smiled at Chris, who did the same in return.

"He helped me make dinner," Chris said, then paused because he didn't want to talk for Pavle.

"I like helping in the kitchen, and I plant lots of flowers." Pavle offering that information was a good sign.

"How chilly is it out? I thought we could eat outside, but I'm not sure if it's warm enough." Late spring evenings could cool off quickly.

"It's a little brisk," Red said.

"Okay. Dining room it is." Chris led them all into the living room before excusing himself to set the table. He hoped leaving Pavle alone wasn't too much for him, but he didn't want to hover and make Pavle feel like a prisoner again. "You husband?" Pavle asked as Chris went into the next room. He was about to turn around to answer, but Terry spoke.

"Yes. Red and I are married. We had the ceremony last year." The smile in Terry's voice came through clearly.

"How you do that?" Pavle asked. "Does everybody...." Thankfully, Terry was patient. "Nobody hate you?" Chris set the silverware on the table, ready to rejoin them.

"Sometimes. But it's okay here. Our marriage is legal. More and more people understand, and it's become much more accepted in the past few years," Terry explained. "Things have changed a lot, and though there is more that needs to happen, we're happy, and we have many good friends, like Chris."

Pavle tilted his head once again. "People know... everyone know?" he asked in what had to be complete disbelief.

"Yes," Red answered. "The people I work with know. Some of them are gay as well, and others are not, but they know. The same for Terry. He is open about who he is." Red put an arm around Terry's shoulder.

"Gay?" Pavle asked, as though rolling the word through his mind for the very first time. "What means... gay?" He blinked and turned to Chris.

"It means men who love other men," Chris explained. Being gay was so much more than that, at least in today's society, but going into the bigger picture at this moment probably wasn't a good idea, so he went for the simple explanation.

"This is okay?" Pavle asked, fear creeping into his voice. His leg shook and his eyes darted around the room the way a small child's do when they don't believe something and desperately need reassurance. He began to shake even more, and Chris wondered if he was okay. He stood as Pavle jumped to his feet and hurried toward the stairs. He raced upward, and Chris watched him go.

"Excuse me," he said quietly to Red and Terry.

"It's all right," Terry reassured him. "All of this could be too much for him." He and Red looked at each other.

"I'll be right back." Chris went up the stairs. Pavle's room was empty, but the bathroom door was closed. Chris knocked gently, and after a few seconds, the door cracked open, Pavle peeking out.

"They are like… me?" he said, blinking, his eyes wet, shaking a little. It took Chris a split second to realize that Pavle had just come out to him.

God, he wanted to take Pavle in his arms and comfort him so badly. But he didn't know if he had the right or if Pavle would accept it. Still, he almost ached to do it. "Yes. Being gay is part of us. It is okay. I am gay too, like Red and Terry." Shit. How stupid could he be? After the situation Pavle had been in, Chris had just assumed that he was gay based upon the situation when he was found. But what if he hadn't been? Chris should have thought of that before. Given the fact that Pavle's free will had been stripped away from him, the distinct possibility that Pavle could have been straight should have been considered. He had been used and hurt, and Chris had made an assumption. "Why don't you come back downstairs and we can get dinner ready." They could find something else to talk about, and Chris needed to be much more careful about topics of conversation. Pavle was here because he needed protection and help. That was all that Chris was supposed to provide.

"Gay not joke?" Pavle asked.

"No, not a joke. It's all right. We'll find something else to talk about if you want." Chris waited for Pavle to come out and go back down the stairs. Then Chris followed, looking anywhere but at Pavle. He needed to keep his mind where it belonged, on his job and not on the stunning example of gentleness that descended the stairs in front of him.

Pavle sat back down, and Chris introduced the subject of swimming. Terry had won gold in the last Olympics, which Pavle seemed to find fascinating. Chris left Pavle with them briefly to check on dinner, then returned and poured some wine as Terry told him all about the thrill of traveling there, and of course all about the race that won him the medal and a level of fame that still carried on.

"I have a photo shoot next week. They want me to model bathing suits."

Red grumbled a little, and Terry patted his hand.

"Red usually goes with me if he can, but this one is when he's on duty. It's only a few days in New York."

"Yeah. But I hate this photographer. He keeps looking...." Red turned beet red, and Chris doubted it was from embarrassment.

"You know you're the only one I care about." Terry's voice was so gentle, and the way he turned to Red, it was clear that photographers—and, well, anyone else for that matter—didn't stand a chance at Terry's heart.

"You love him?" Pavle asked Terry.

Red was rough and had had a hard life, or at least his face read that way. A few scars and the beard gave him a hard look, but as soon as he turned to Terry, all that disappeared when he smiled. Red's expression lit up, and when Terry nodded and took Red's hand, Chris felt as though he were looking into a private moment.

Pavle must have felt the same. He turned away and cleared his throat. "I help with dinner." He went into the kitchen.

"Is he really okay?" Terry asked.

"I think so. He gets a little overwhelmed at times, and I think he's finding the concept that being gay isn't bad a little world-rocking."

"Go see to him. Red and I will be fine." Terry picked up his glass of wine and took a sip. "If it's okay, he and I can go wander out in the yard. It's so beautiful this time of year."

"Even more so. Pavle loves flowers." Chris led them through the house, past where Pavle was making a salad in the kitchen. He stiffened as they walked by but didn't look up. Red and Terry went outside, and Chris returned to the kitchen.

"You need to explain what's going on," Chris said as gently as he could. "I can't help you if I don't understand."

Pavle looked up from chopping lettuce into small pulverized bits, and sniffed. "I do not understand. Everything is different here. I not know if good or bad."

"Everything isn't good or bad. Sometimes things are just different." God, Chris hoped he was helping, but he wasn't making a huge amount of sense, even to himself. "Just tell me what you're trying to wrestle with."

"Them." Pavle pointed out the back, and Chris turned, looking through the other room and out into the garden as Red gently cupped Terry's cheeks and kissed him. "They... not shame."

Chris paused a second as his brain nearly slipped a cog as a connection he'd never considered slipped into place. He and Pavle most definitely needed to have a very in-depth talk. "No. They are happy." He gently took the knife and set it aside, carefully taking Pavle's hand.

"Is there anything Red and I can do?" Terry asked.

Chris jumped a little. He hadn't heard them come back in, he was so intent on what he hoped Pavle was going to tell him. Abandoning his chance to speak with Pavle alone, he sighed and realized this mess was his own fault. He should have waited and made sure Pavle was ready to meet people before he pressed it on him. "It's almost ready. But maybe Red would like to grill the steaks."

"Sure." Red took the plate and returned to the backyard.

"I go sit too?" Pavle asked.

"Sure."

Pavle hurried outside as well, and Chris hoped it was to help Red, but Pavle sat on the opposite side of the garden, in the sun, face to the sky, lips moving as though he were talking to someone.

"He's a strange one," Terry said from next to him. There was no heat in it, just an observation. "I suppose he has a right to be. It's hard for me to understand what he's been through."

"For any of us." Chris brought some of the food to the table. "Pavle doesn't like to talk about it. He's answered FBI questions, and those stories were enough to have me seeing red." He recalled that day and his ripping the chair apart. "He hasn't talked about what happened since. I wonder if he's trying to put it behind him, and I can't blame him. I know I sure as hell would." But there were so many other things that Chris wanted to know about him.

"You really care for him," Terry said. "It's there whenever you talk about him. Hell, I mentioned that he seemed strange and you looked ready to bite my head off, your eyes blazing for a second." He took a step back so he could see him better. "I didn't mean anything by the comment."

"It doesn't matter what I feel for him." Chris squared his shoulders and stood a little taller. "I'm supposed to protect him and make sure he's okay to make his court appearances. I have to…."

"Oh, bullshit…." Terry cut right through the start of Chris's dutiful monologue. "You like him, and you can say what you will, but the heart wants what the heart wants…. Denying it only makes it harder. If you like him, admit it and move forward. Because Lord knows, Pavle deserves someone who truly cares about him."

"But it's a minefield." If he allowed his emotions to go down that road, Chris was only setting himself up to be hurt. He was well aware that the end game was for Pavle to eventually go home. And there were ethical issues as well. He was supposed to be protecting Pavle, not falling for him. That was how these cases ended… at least as far as he knew. What Pavle wanted was what was important, not Chris.

"Maybe. Even if it is, doesn't Pavle still deserve whatever happiness comes his way? And for him to choose what he wants?"

Terry's logic was unassailable and exactly how Chris felt. Why else would the thought of Pavle returning home eventually make his stomach clench? But it shouldn't at all. Pavle was a work assignment. He was someone who had been taken advantage of, and God in heaven, Chris had let him work his way into his heart without even trying. He was completely screwed, and there was nothing he could do about it.

"He does." And his own feelings and petty worries be damned.

"The steaks are about done." Red brought in the plate from the raw meat, and Chris placed it in the sink and got a fresh one for him. "Is he all right? He just sits out there." Red motioned toward the back.

"He spent a long time not able to see the sun." Chris's mind went back to that dank room that smelled of rot and mold. "I think he needs it. Just like I think he needs pretty things. He planted most of the flowers out there, and he'd plant more if I had room for them." It tickled Chris's green-thumbed heart that Pavle loved plants so much.

Red nodded. "As long as he's okay." He returned outside, and when he came back in, Pavle followed and they all took places at the table.

Pavle ate with his usual quickness, but unlike other times, he barely spoke, though Chris noticed him watching quite a bit.

"What was your home like, before you came here?" Terry asked.

"Small." Pavle made a motion with his fingers. "Town small, and I know all." He set down his fork. "Mama and Papa grow things."

"They were farmers?" Terry asked.

Pavle nodded. "Small. We have food, but no else. Mama…." He hummed and mimed sewing. "They dead," he added.

"I'm sorry," Terry said, and Pavle shrugged.

"I miss them, when dark and I go to sleep, but they far away now." He picked up his fork and returned to eating as though he hadn't just said one of the saddest things Chris had ever heard. Chris supposed the loss of his mom and dad paled in comparison to years of captivity and threats. Pavle continued eating, and Chris had no idea what else to say. "I here now. Things be different? Yes?"

"Yes. I will try to make sure things are different now," Chris promised him. It was the best he could do.

"Of course they will be," Terry said with a smile. "You're here now. You can try to build your own life."

Chris wished it were that easy. If Pavle decided to stay—and with so many things foreign to him, that was probably a big if—there were many hoops that he'd have to go through. That was probably another conversation he and Marie needed to have with him. There was going to come a time, probably quite soon, when he was going to have to decide what he wanted. Obstacles—right now Chris saw only obstacles, and he needed to try to change his outlook somehow.

His phone vibrated in his pocket. Chris pulled it out and excused himself, answering Marie's call.

"Is Pavle all right?" she asked barely after he'd said hello.

"Yes. Why? It's been quiet here." Other than the feeling earlier that he was being watched, but that could have been caused by anyone, and he'd not seen anything unusual. "What's happened?"

"Pavle's first safe house, the one he didn't feel comfortable in because it was all men, they received a visit from two men in police uniforms saying they were there to inspect the place and review the cases of everyone there. The caretaker called me, and I called Carlisle Police because they said they were with them. No one was sent out, and no one ever would be… not like that. We manage the homes, and the police work through us. Marvin is huge and he didn't let them in. When he told them more officers were on the way, they took off, but only when the sirens sounded."

"Jesus…." Chris groaned. "Do you need me to try to dig into anything? Red, one of the officers, is here with his husband for dinner. I can ask him what they found out."

"Marvin got their license plates and provided descriptions, but I just know they were after Pavle. We have many safe houses, and the only ones that are bothered have been the ones where Pavle has stayed."

"Okay. Right now he's safe. I've been keeping an eye out and limiting my contact to just one person in the department." He hadn't trusted anyone at the department beyond Briggs with information on where he was. "Would you be able to review who has access to your system? If you think someone is using that system to get their information, then there might be someone with access who shouldn't have it."

Marie hummed softly. "I thought of that and did the review last week. I removed some old accesses, but they hadn't actually used the system in a while."

"This lapse is new, so I bet either it's someone with new access or someone whose access has been compromised. Maybe check for increased activity on an account."

"That's not a bad idea. I'll also go through the logs for specific information access, thought that's going to be much more difficult. The logs are pretty intense. But I'll try."

"Let me know if you find anything. I'll let Briggs know what's going on, and maybe he can help from his end. Maybe Red can help as well." Chris didn't want to expand the circle too greatly, but they didn't seem to know where Pavle was and were trying to flush him out.

"Okay. If I find anything, I'll call."

Chris agreed that he'd do the same and ended the call, returning to the dining room, where three sets of eyes followed him.

"What wrong?" Pavle asked.

"An incident at one of the safe houses today," Chris answered.

"I heard about that. Do you think it's related to Pavle?" Red asked.

"Marie thinks so. But I don't know what they expected to get. He isn't in the system, and even if they got very far, none of the people there know where he is." Chris turned to Pavle. "None of us is going to let anything happen to you. They called the police, who went right over."

Red humphed softly. "They aren't going to find him unless they get lucky, and we can't allow that to happen. I'll check things out quietly. A lot of the guys are friends, and I'll see if they have any ideas."

"It's organized crime. They have a bigger reach than any of us would like to think is possible," Chris explained, and Red nodded his agreement.

Pavle sat quietly, his eyes as big as saucers. "People hurt because of me."

"No. People are getting hurt because bad people are doing the hurting," Terry said. "This is not your fault. Right, Red?"

"Yes. This isn't your fault. Chris needs to keep you safe, and I need to work with my colleagues to try to find these people. This has got to stop soon or we aren't going to be able to keep anyone safe." Red picked up his dishes and carried them into the kitchen.

"There's beer in the refrigerator if you want one," Chris called, and the refrigerator door opened and closed. Red brought a couple of extras with him, and even Pavle took one.

"We know there's a leak somewhere in one of the departments, and I think it's mine," Chris said. "Briggs thinks so too, but he isn't getting very far."

"The new sheriff is…." Red tipped his bottle to his lips. "He's something else."

"The guy is a moron. And he's going to run for a full term. Someone needs to run against him, but everyone in my department is too scared to do it. If they lose, they'll be out of a job." Chris gulped down his beer. "I so want him to be the leak, but if he really is, then…." He looked at the others. "He can't be. The sheriff doesn't know exactly where Pavle is, but he probably has an idea. He assigned me to protect him." As much as he didn't like his new boss, at least he wasn't in with the mob. That was some comfort anyway.

"Politics stinks," Terry pronounced. "I avoid it as much as possible."

Red slipped his arm around Terry's shoulder. "No one can avoid it. Remember the presentation and hoops you had to jump through to get the funding for the pool improvements? All of that is politics, just on a smaller scale."

Red and Terry talked about the projects Terry was working on in order to get the facilities at the Y upgraded. Chris was relieved that the conversation had shifted, and from the way Pavle listened and watched them, sitting back in his chair, he was relieved not to be the center of everyone's attention as well.

Chris eventually cleared the last of the dishes and got another beer. They moved to the living room and talked for another hour before the conversation slowed.

"Your mama know about you?" Pavle asked out of the blue, but Chris was willing to bet he'd been trying to figure out how to ask his question for a while.

"My mom and dad are dead. But my aunt Margaret, who raised me afterward, knows. She loves Terry." Red drew him a little closer. Those two were still so much in love with each other, it was impossible not to see it.

"You not shame?" Pavle asked. The others didn't seem to understand his question, at least not fully. But another piece of the enigma that was Pavle fell into place for Chris.

"No. We aren't ashamed of being together," Terry answered, but that wasn't Pavle's question.

Chris turned to him. "Pavle, there is no shame in being gay... not here. Yes, some people don't understand and don't like gay people, but there is no shame in it. I'm gay, and so are Red and Terry. The people we work with know we're gay. Terry is respected and known around the country. In most places in this country, you can be gay, and that's okay. There is no shame in it, and it's not bad or nasty. It's just part of who we are." He glanced at the others, who were both nodding.

The disbelief written in Pavle's narrowed eyes and the creases around his mouth said he didn't completely believe him. "But...."

Red nudged Terry and finished the last of his beer. "I think Terry and I should be going." He stood and carried the bottles to the kitchen. He and Terry said good night to both of them and thanked Chris for the evening and the dinner. After hugs and walking to the door, Chris saw them out.

He gathered the dishes, loaded the dishwasher, and got it running before making sure the house was locked up and turning out the lights.

He found Pavle on the sofa in the living room, feet on the floor, back straight, hands folded in his lap, blinking as Chris came in and sat in the chair across from him. "You must have questions."

Pavle nodded once. "It really okay to love men? Like they?"

Chris nodded. "Is that what you meant when you said you were ashamed?" He had thought it was because of what Pavle had done or been forced to do over the last four years, but now he was wondering if the shame welled up because of how he felt. Because he was gay in the first place.

"I shame all over," Pavle said softly, and without thinking, Chris shifted to the sofa next to him. He stayed quiet, hoping Pavle would explain. "I stupid."

"No. You aren't stupid. You were taken advantage of and it wasn't your fault. They lied to you all the time." Honestly, Chris wasn't sure what to try to tackle first. He took a deep breath. "Why don't you tell me why you are shame." He purposely used Pavle's term in order to try to draw out his meaning.

"I like they… like you," Pavle said, turning toward Chris with tears running down his cheeks. "Back home, they hate me. I shame my family. Mama and Papa hate me if know." He slashed away the tears with a brusque hand movement. "They hate me." His shoulders bounced, and he leaned against Chris, who put his arms around him.

"Your mama and papa loved you." While Chris didn't know that, it seemed to be what Pavle needed to hear. "When I was young, I told my mom and dad that I was gay. I thought they would hate me too. It took a long time for me to get up enough courage to tell them, but when I did, they said they already knew. That they had figured it out for themselves and they loved me." Chris closed his eyes, rocking him gently back and forth.

"But I shame my village," Pavle whispered.

"Did they know about you?" Chris asked, and Pavle shook his head against him.

"I leave. Come to America. I never tell." The words could barely be heard through the agony that seemed to be welling up from inside. Chris tried to imagine what Pavle was feeling at that moment and failed completely. "I cannot tell. I fear and shame."

Chris had no words that could comfort him. Instead, Chris held him, wishing for all the world that Pavle didn't have to go through this.

"Am I shame?" Chris finally asked.

Pavle looked up from Chris's chest, his blue shirt dotted with darker spots from the release of Pavle's hurt. "You strong and smart. You no shame." He sniffed.

"But I'm like you. I'm gay too." Maybe he had hit on something. "If you are shame, then I am shame too because we are the same. We are both gay and like other men." He held Pavle's gaze, hoping he could get the message through to him one way or another.

"But you different," Pavle whispered.

"How am I different?" Chris challenged. "Yes, I wasn't brought here and treated the way you were. Now you can be sad—you can be angry at the men who did that." He gently rubbed Pavle's back. "You can want revenge on them and try to hurt them back—all that seems reasonable to me. But being ashamed of yourself only lets them win." He titled Pavle's head upward until their gazes met, his deep brown eyes meeting Chris's. "I want you to have a chance at happiness, and you aren't going to do that if you're ashamed of who you are."

Pavle blinked. "How know how stop?" Pavle looked at him with so much trust in his eyes, looking to Chris for guidance and help. In those few seconds, he seemed innocent and a little lost, but determined to understand. Yes… determination seemed to win out over the rest, and it built like a slow fire in Pavle's eyes.

A bubble of heat built around Chris, centering on Pavle and the way he seemed to have built a fire so close to him. Chris knew he shouldn't even think that, but his body had already reacted, and he'd positioned his leg so Pavle didn't feel him. Damn it all, the last thing he wanted was for Pavle to think Chris was interested in him for sex. No, that was so wrong. Chris would have loved nothing more than to take Pavle upstairs to his bed and make love to him all night long. To show him just how beautiful things could be between people who cared for each other. He could demonstrate that there was truly nothing to be ashamed of for hours.

In his dreams, he sometimes saw himself holding Pavle's hand as they walked together through the backyard filled with friends and loved ones. In those snippets that his mind conjured up, he was always smiling and occasionally looked at where they held each other just to prove it was real. Of course, it wasn't, and he'd wake up, a little lost as the reality of his lonely life washed back over him again.

"You need to figure that out for yourself." God, that sounded so stupid and like psychological mumbo jumbo. But it was true and part of what he hoped Pavle was working through in therapy. "I can't do it for you. But I can tell you that here, in this house, you have nothing to be ashamed of… ever. You get to be yourself, and you don't have to worry about anyone telling you anything different."

"What about Marie?" he asked quietly.

Chris chuckled and blinked. "Nothing would make Marie happier than you being happy. I know that. She wants that just as much as I do." His heart raced and his skin tingled everywhere Pavle touched him. Attraction and need grew by the second, and Chris felt his will-power, the ability to resist Pavle, slipping away. But he had to. This was not something he could do, nor was it something Pavle necessarily wanted. Sweat broke out on his brow as Chris gently and slowly moved away. "You need to be happy. I will help you as best I can. Know that you can tell me anything you need to, and I'll do my best to help get you what you need." If it was in his power to make Pavle happy, he'd do it.

Chris got to his feet because he needed some distance between them, afraid Pavle would see just what he'd done to him. No matter how wrong his body's reaction was, he could do nothing to stop it. Pavle set off a firestorm inside him. Wrong or not, it had happened, and he needed some time to think.

"I go outside?" Pavle asked, and Chris nodded.

"Turn on the lights in the garden so you can see." Chris watched Pavle leave the room, and he waited a few minutes to catch his breath before going to work in the kitchen. He'd intended to finish the cleanup in the morning, but now was as good a time as any, and it would give him something to do besides think about Pavle.

Chris finished the dishes, his mind still circling with contradictions regarding Pavle. There was only one decision to make, and that was for him to either resolve to keep their relationship professional, or return to work and back out of the assignment. The sheriff wouldn't be happy, and God knows he'd probably find himself back on duty at the jail before he could turn around. So he'd be professional and forget the ideas that kept creeping into his head.

He turned out the lights the same way he was determined to turn off that part of himself that kept thinking about Pavle, and made his way to the back room.

The floods were on in the yard, the flowers awash in light. Pavle wandered the path to the garage, turned, and came toward the house. Chris silently opened the window for fresh air and sat in his chair, a steady stream of Serbian floating to his ears. While Chris had no idea what Pavle was saying, his agitated tone needed no translation. He continued pacing, talking to himself, sometimes louder and other times barely a mutter, but always with an earnestness and plaintive tone to his words.

He sat back, watching Pavle, until movement on the other side of the fence caught his attention. Chris stiffened and sat forward, watching as the shadows moved again. He jumped out of his seat and ran outside. Pavle approached him, and Chris motioned him toward the door, putting his finger to his lips. Pavle looked at him over his shoulder as he went inside.

When Pavle was inside, Chris came close to where he'd seen the movement and jumped up on the bench to peer over. "John, what are you doing?" Chris asked when he saw his neighbor trying to climb a tree in his yard. John's foot slipped off the limb and he nearly fell to the concrete walkway below, scrambling for a few seconds before lowering himself to the ground.

"Is that some Russian over there?" John demanded as though that made his actions justified. He was one of those conspiracy theory guys. The last time Chris had invited him and his wife over during the summer for a party, he had talked Chris's ear off about left-wing conspiracies and how they wanted to suppress his right to carry a gun. Frankly, the thought of John with a gun was enough to keep him awake at night.

"I have a guest staying with me who doesn't speak a great deal of English. If you had questions, you could have asked." Chris lifted himself upward, staring at John. "I am a deputy with the sheriff's department. I don't think you need to worry about who is staying at my house." Chris wished he could say the same thing about his neighbors. The stuff he'd heard drifting over the fence had been enough on occasion to curl his hair.

"I was just checking," John defended, crossing his arms over his chest. "I have a right to keep my home protected."

"Yes, you do." Chris hardened his features. "But if you want to snoop on me, then maybe I'll take more of an interest in what's going on over here." He held John's gaze and let his message sink in. He didn't tell John that he'd installed cameras to watch his backyard from both the house and the garage. They weren't positioned specifically so he could see his neighbors, but there was some bleed-over.

Chris stepped back and down onto his side of the fence, then went back inside, setting the lights to motion sensor and closing the door.

He looked around for Pavle, going from room to room, but didn't find him. Chris continued upstairs, but he wasn't in his bedroom. "Pavle," he called, keeping his voice gentle, even as he wondered what could have happened to him. Chris retraced his steps back through the house and finally found Pavle crouched behind his chair.

"I no Russian," Pavle said softly. "He say I Russian. I no."

"I know that." Chris gently took Pavle's arm and guided him to his feet. "He heard you talking and let his imagination take over. John is a little weird sometimes."

"Okay. I no Russian and no like Russians. They hurt us long time." The level of resentment and anger in Pavle's voice surprised him. Not that it was there, but its ferocity. Pavle sometimes got scared, but up until now, he hadn't shown this kind of negativity about anyone other than the people who'd hurt him.

"All right. He had no right to say that. But you're safe here." Chris realized as soon as he said it that Pavle wasn't going to understand. "He isn't going to hurt you."

"Why he climb tree?" Pavle asked.

"He's nosey," Chris answered.

"What nosey mean?" Pavle asked, feeling his own nose like there was something wrong with it.

"He was curious. He wanted to know why he was hearing you speak and he couldn't understand it. I told him to mind his own business." Chris motioned for Pavle to sit down. "Sometimes people say things that might scare you. But you can always ask me about it, okay? You don't have to hide or run away." He let that sink in. "What did you think was going to happen?"

"That he bad." Pavle swallowed hard. "One who took me, he talk like him."

"You mean with an accent?" Chris asked.

Pavle nodded. "I think he come for me. But he no him? Then he say I Russian...."

"It's okay. I'm not mad, but you don't need to be afraid all the time. John hasn't lived there for very long, but I'm pretty sure he got the house from his mom and dad."

"I know no him, but...."

Chris did know. "It's okay to be scared sometimes."

"I scared all time. I scared when someone knock on door. I think they come take me away. When it dark, I listen. He... master... he come at night... he drink...." Pavle shook a little. "But he gone now. I know he gone.

He scared too." Sometimes Pavle was incredibly insightful. "I think he leave because I know him."

"Yes. He's afraid of you and what you could say about him." Chris knew that was right, and he needed to talk to Briggs in the morning to find out if they had made any progress in apprehending the guy who had held him in town. It had been a while... almost too long, and law enforcement needed to bring his most recent captor to justice. Right now they were failing Pavle and the others in his position. Chris knew that sometimes things took time, but he was well aware that the more time passed, the more likely it was that the asshole had skipped town and possibly the state. "He isn't going to get near you without coming through me first."

"I free from him. That means I have power now." Pavle stood a little straighter.

"Yes. You do. What you know means you have power. But it also means that others want to stop you from telling what you know." There were two sides to every coin, and Pavle had to understand all of it.

Pavle nodded. "But I no Russian," he said, raising his head.

Chris put his hands up in surrender. "You not Russian." He smiled, and Pavle returned it. "I never thought you were."

Pavle turned toward the fence Chris shared with John. "He jerk."

"Sometimes." Chris couldn't help smiling. Maybe he and Pavle were watching too much television. Sometimes Pavle picked up the most interesting words.

"And nosey," Pavle added with a smile, pointing to his nose and then motioning for it to grow. "Big nosey."

"Yes." Chris loved that Pavle's sense of humor was beginning to show through. Some of his fear that had been a constant in his life for so long seemed to be receding, with some of Pavle's natural personality shining through.

Pavle shifted his weight from foot to foot.

"Why are you nervous?" Chris asked.

Pavle shrugged. "I not know." He continued rocking from side to side. "Maybe I go bed. Think about it."

Chris watched him go and shook his head slightly. There were times when he wished he truly understood Pavle and could read his mind. But then again, the things he'd find there would probably send chills of fear running down his back. Pavle had seen and experienced the darkest parts of humanity, and that left an impression—it changed a person.

"Good night," Chris said, and began turning out the last of the lights as he went through the house before going upstairs. As he reached his room, the bathroom door opened and Pavle stepped out in a pair of sleep shorts, on his way to his room. His bare chest was pale, exposing his slightness, his ribs still showing at his sides. Chris swallowed hard and tried not to stare. Anger warred with desire for a few seconds, until he turned away toward his room. "I'll see you in the morning." He swallowed once again and closed the door behind him.

How thin Pavle still was sent an aching throb through his head. He should make sure to add extra food to Pavle's plates to help ensure he grew stronger and healthier. More worrisome was the fact that the image of him shirtless lingered in Chris's mind well after he'd closed the bedroom door. But he was beautiful, and even though he was slight, there was a strength in him that carried through in the way he walked and held himself now. He wasn't hunched and no longer tried to make himself seem small. Pavle had a presence around him, and that was attractive and drew Chris to him like a moth to flame.

"Damn, I'm so messed up." And when he closed his eyes to push away the image, it only intensified.

# CHAPTER 6

HIS PHONE rang next to the bed, and Chris blinked awake. He rolled over, grabbed the phone to silence it, and checked the screen. He groaned when he saw it was from the station. "Hello?"

"It's Briggs."

Chris forced his mind to work. "What's going on?"

"We got him." Briggs actually sounded happy. "Harvey Anthony is sitting in jail at this moment, and you're not going to believe this. He was picked up at a hotel in the Poconos with his wife and kids. It seems he told them he'd been on an extended business trip for the last few weeks and then asked them to meet him at the hotel. The state police picked him up for us."

"Oh, God. Did his family have any idea?" Chris felt for them.

"I don't think so. The wife went nuts. Apparently when they told her what they were arresting her husband for, she threatened to cut off his manhood and shove it down his throat." Briggs was definitely taking some delight in all this. "Anyway, I wanted to let you know, and we're going to arrange a viewing so Pavle can formally identify him. Then we can put our part of this case behind us."

"Our part?" Chris asked.

"That's what the sheriff said. The rest of the case is the jurisdiction of the state and FBI. I think he plans to turn Pavle over to them and—"

Chris growled. "The hell he is. Pavle isn't some piece of property or something he can stick in an evidence locker." The more he interacted with the new sheriff, the more he came to hate the man.

"I agree with you, so I put a call in to the FBI and they agree as well." Damn, Briggs was sneaky. "They want Pavle kept right where he is for now."

"The boss is going to have your head if he finds out you went around him." Chris liked Briggs, but his esteem for the man jumped considerably. "I won't say a thing. You know that. Just let me know when I need to have Pavle at the station."

"I'll take him in. You're on leave, remember? I don't want anyone to see you here right now. I'll let you know where to meet me, and then I'll return him to your house when we're done." He yawned. "I'm beginning to narrow down our leak. I believe it's here, but I'm not getting anywhere fast. Three deputies and the sheriff were given access to the Social Services housing database within the last week. Their access was supposed to be specific and for a limited time, and it's now been revoked again, as it should be."

"But you think one of them tried to look up where Pavle was?"

"That's the theory I'm working under right now."

Chris stretched. "I'll have Marie get in touch with you directly. She maintains that system and can probably help you get more information pretty quickly, especially if you know who to look for."

"Good. Text me the information, and I'll call her in the morning." Briggs yawned again.

"Have you been home yet?" Chris checked the time again, groaning softly. That was Briggs. When he was on the trail of something, he was like a bulldog and didn't give up, even at three in the morning.

"I'm on my way out now. It's easier to work on this when nobody is here. I'll call about nine to make arrangements." He ended the call.

Chris sent Briggs Marie's contact information. He also sent her a message that Briggs was going to be in touch, figuring she would see it in the morning.

*What's happened?* Marie texted back.

*Don't you sleep either?* he sent her.

*Insomnia.*

Okay. Apparently no one slept. *They got the man who was holding Pavle. He's in custody. Briggs is going to take Pavle in for identification. He'll also work with you to help determine who might be using your system improperly. He has people he wants to look into.* He sent a smiley face because all this was good news. Progress was good.

*Awesome. I'll be glad to work with him. How is Pavle?*

*Doing better, I think. Coming to grips with a few things. Maybe you can stop by if you're careful not to be seen. I have some things to ask you. And you can talk to him. He asks about you.*

*Be there tomorrow afternoon.* She sent a smiley face, and Chris returned one, then set his phone on the nightstand before trying to go back to sleep.

"Chris." Pavle's muffled voice barely reached his ears, followed by a soft knock.

Chris got up, slipping on the blue robe he'd slung over the back of his chair before opening the door.

"Can't you sleep?" he asked. Pavle wore shorts and one of Chris's old T-shirts, which hung on him. Chris's heart did a little flutter.

"I hear you talking. I hear my name." He wiped his eyes and shuffled inside a few steps before stopping. "I no sleep."

"Okay." Chris sat on the edge of the bed. "They caught Harvey Anthony, and he's in jail right now. Deputy Briggs is going to take you to identify him. He will not be able to see you, and all you have to do is say if he's really the man who held you here. That's all. After that Briggs will bring you back. There is no way Anthony can hurt you, and you need to be strong, if you can."

Pavle nodded. "I be strong."

"Good. Marie will come over tomorrow afternoon to talk to you. She wants to see how you're doing. Okay? Briggs is a good man and he will look after you."

"Why you no come?" Pavle asked. "Want you there."

"No one at the department knows where you are. They think I am on family leave, and we don't want anyone to know anything different. So they cannot see me. I am going to bring you to Briggs, and he will drive you back here. If you want, I can make sure Marie is there." He wished so very much that he could go along with Pavle, but it was for his ultimate safety. Chris patted the space next to him, and Pavle sat on the edge of the bed. "You are strong enough that you can do this. I know you can." He took Pavle's hand.

"Want make you… pride," he said softly. "Want you… like me."

"Pavle, I already like you, and I am so proud of you. I can't tell you how much." Chris swallowed hard. "I see people every day who give up. You don't. That makes you strong." He squeezed Pavle's fingers gently.

"You say I need know what I want." Pavle spoke slowly. "I know what I want." He looked at where their hands joined. "This. Want always have this." He raised their hands together. "I want stay here. Be here… with you. I want this."

Chris was taken aback. Did Pavle understand what he was asking? "You want to live here with me?" He swallowed hard. What Pavle said could have so many meanings, and Chris wasn't sure if it was what Pavle meant or what he thought it meant.

"I want this." Pavle squeezed Chris's hand harder, then slipped off the bed and leaned in quickly to kiss him. "I want…."

Chris held his breath. Pavle had kissed him, gently, quickly.

He shook his head to clear it. "How about we go back to bed and we can talk about this in the morning. Okay?" Chris needed to think, and he certainly wasn't going to take a single kiss as a declaration of love. It could mean so many different things, especially in light of what had happened to Pavle. It didn't matter that Chris's heart beat faster just having Pavle near and the kiss sent his temperature soaring. None of that mattered. All that mattered was that Pavle had the chance to be happy and to make his own choices for his life.

Pavle let go of Chris's hand. "We talk later," he said with more force than Chris expected, and left the room.

Chris went to close the door, shaking his head and wondering how he could possibly get any more sleep tonight.

AFTER A good breakfast, Chris took Pavle to where Briggs had agreed to meet them.

"You be strong. I know you can do it." He squeezed Pavle's hand once he'd pulled to a stop. Briggs opened the passenger door and escorted Pavle to the other car. Chris waved goodbye and pulled away once Briggs had driven off.

He sighed, wondering what he was going to do for a few hours. Chris decided to go to the grocery store and run some errands. He had to be careful not to be seen by someone in the department, so after making a few stops and unloading the groceries at home, he drove to Nanna's.

"Where's Pavle?" she asked as soon as she opened the door, looking around.

"He's with the police." Chris kissed her cheek and stepped inside. He explained about last night's arrest and why he was staying away.

"Are you hungry?" Nanna asked.

"I had breakfast. Why don't you sit down and I'll make us some tea?" She always tried to do so much.

He went to the kitchen and put the water on, setting up the pot and cups, then carried a tray back into the living room. He poured her tea and handed it to her.

"Do you want to tell me what's going on with you?" she pressed as she took the cup.

"Nothing. Everything is good. Pavle is doing well. He seems to be getting used to things, but still eats like he was starving, which I think he might have been. Pavle has planted my backyard full of flowers, and tomorrow we're going to see the people who helped rescue him. A minister and his wife." He sat back and sipped from the cup. Chris didn't love tea, but he'd learned to drink it with Nanna.

Nanna shook her head. "Have you listened to yourself? I asked how you were, and all you talk about is

Pavle." She set her cup and saucer on the coffee table, the same one Chris remembered playing on as a child. "Not that he isn't a sweet boy, but I think your answer tells me plenty."

"I've protecting him for a while. He's been staying in my house, and…."

Nanna shook her head. "There's more than that. I might be old, but I'm not blind. You like that boy." She leaned closer. "He's touched your heart. Not that there's anything wrong with that."

Chris scoffed. "Nanna. He's someone I'm supposed to be protecting, not falling in love with. What happens when this is all over and he decides to go home? Or worse, what if he isn't allowed to stay? You know how things are right now with that sort of thing." He set his cup across from hers.

"What does Pavle say he wants? Have you asked him?" She looked at him over her nose, the same look he'd gotten when he'd trampled her peas in the garden as a kid. "Of course you haven't." She sighed with exasperation. "You were always so careful around everyone else that we wondered if you'd ever learn to say what you wanted… and you're doing it again. You care for Pavle, so you're puzzling through everything trying to figure out what he wants."

Chris rolled his eyes. "What am I supposed to do? I won't press Pavle into anything—and I could do that. He likes me, I know he does, and I like him. Pavle is a really nice man, but he's been through hell—you know that. What if he wants to make me happy and ends up in a relationship he doesn't want?" He huffed and snatched up his cup with enough force that it almost spilled everywhere.

"But what if he does? And what do you want?" she said, so damned calm.

"He's been through so much. I can't foist myself on him no matter how I feel."

"Foisting…." She snorted. "I like that word. But you, my dear, have never been a foister. You'd sit back and let Pavle walk out of your life without saying a word. That sweet young man has had all that's good and kind stripped away from him, and look at him… he's kind and thoughtful. He still cares about everyone else, when a lot of people would be selfish or spend their time feeling sorry for themselves."

"He's never done that."

"Nope. But he is trying to figure things out and he's looking to you to help him."

"Yeah. But that doesn't mean he loves me. And can I really expect him to simply form a relationship with me when he hasn't had a chance to see anything of the world? That isn't fair to him. He needs to have the chance to experience things and be able to make decisions that affect his life." Chris blinked and sipped the tea.

"Yes, he does. But what I want to ask you is, if Pavle actually tells you what he wants, will you listen with your heart as well as that stubborn head of yours, or will you hang on to what you think?" She leaned forward and guided his cup to the table. "Sweetheart, sometimes you get so deep in your own head that you don't listen to what others are trying to tell you. If Pavle says what he wants, he isn't going to beat you over the head." She rolled her eyes and patted his cheek. "He's going to tell you much more subtly and in his own way."

"Like by kissing me?" Chris asked, and immediately wished he'd kept his mouth shut.

"He kissed you?" Nanna asked. "That must have taken a lot of courage. You need to talk to him, listen to him, and believe him when he tells you what he wants. The man knows his own mind. He might have some trouble expressing himself in English, but that doesn't mean he doesn't know what he wants, only that he may have difficulty expressing it to you."

"Then what do I do?" Chris asked. "Have you move into the house, so you can translate for me?" He was being ridiculous and regretted it immediately, and the momentary "biting a lemon" look on Nanna's lips showed pretty clearly how she felt.

"I love you, honey, but we'd hate each other in a few days." She chuckled. "I like doing things my way, and so do you. Besides, when my callers come to visit, we'd want some privacy." She winked at him, and Chris nearly dropped his cup. The last thing he wanted to think about was his nanna dating… and having callers. Who knew what that meant? He needed brain bleach, and he needed it bad. There was no way he was ever going to be able to unhear that. "I'm old, but not dead, you know." She sipped her tea while Chris tried his best not to choke.

"You can be as undead as you'd like, but that doesn't mean I want to hear about you bumping uglies with some old man." He shivered and closed his eyes, shoving away the terrifying images that tried to push their way into his head.

She snorted. "You know Richie Haskins from next door?" Now she was just being mean.

"Nanna, I don't need to know. Really, please. Just let me go through life thinking that you're my perfect nanna who never has sex with anyone and is loving and caring and completely celibate. It means I can sleep at night." His head pounded, and he drank the last of his cup of tea. "I think we got off the topic." Something he swore he was going to regret for days and days.

"Don't worry, honey. I read this article about a resurgence in STDs among older people, so I make him wrap his willie." She set her cup on the table, and Chris knew she was doing it on purpose now.

Okay. Time for a little payback. "Thank God. Can you imagine me having to take you to the clap clinic?" He rolled his eyes and actually managed to catch his breath, though the idea of Nanna with a venereal disease left him cold. "Anyway... you were saying... about Pavle? Before the conversation fell into the abyss leading halfway to hell."

"Oh, yes." She smiled as though they'd been talking about puppies and kittens. "You need to listen to him, really listen. Not police listen, like you're interrogating someone, but using your ears as well as your heart."

"But...." Chris sighed, having trouble putting his thoughts together. It had to be an errant image of Nanna with her neighbor going at it. He shook his head to try to get the idea out of his mind, but it wasn't fucking working.

"Just trust yourself and your heart." She sat back slowly. "All kidding about my love life aside, you have an amazing heart, and you want me and Pavle to be happy. You always wanted to make others happy. It's part of your DNA. So listen to him and worry a little bit less about what you think is good for him and what you think he needs. Let him tell you. That boy had a long time to think and to dream about what his life would be like when his nightmares were over. Sometimes he didn't dare think about it because he was so busy trying to survive, but he did dream, and Pavle knows what he wants."

"Has he told you?" Chris asked.

Nanna shook her head. "Pavle is smart enough to make up his own mind. You said he kissed you. Do you think Pavle would really do that if he wasn't trying to tell you something?" She shifted in her chair. "Getting old sucks," she added with a slight wince.

"I keep wondering what he meant. I mean...." He closed his eyes, willing the start of a headache away.

"Think about it. For years Pavle had no control over who he kissed or who he had sex with. That choice was taken away from him. But last night, he voluntarily kissed you. You didn't ask or tell him to—he just did it... right?"

"I guess. But.... A kiss is...." He hated when he couldn't find the words.

"Sometimes the most intimate thing we as humans can do. I know you might think it's sex, but I think it's a kiss. Sex, at least in Pavle's world, was traded—it was payment. But a kiss, that's the window to the heart... and soul. It always was for me... still is."

Chris nodded slowly. He had to agree with that. "But it can be something else entirely."

"Yes, but a kiss, freely given, unasked for... that is something special. It's a glimpse and small peek into his heart." She leaned forward to pat Chris's knee. "You need to sit down and talk with him." She paused. "And then you have to be honest and tell him how you feel. That is often the more difficult side of the conversation."

"I can't. Not right now. If I tell Pavle how I feel about him, he'll want to make me happy and probably go along with what I want. He feels indebted to me, and I won't use that against him in any way. No matter what anyone says." He took a deep breath and released it. "All this might be putting the horse before the cart anyway." Chris jumped when his phone vibrated. It was Briggs.

"Pavle did great. We're finishing up here, and I'll drop him at your house, around the back, in half an hour."

Chris acknowledged that and slipped his phone in his pocket. "I need to go." A touch of anxiety was already building in his stomach. "They finished at the police station." He took care of Nanna's cup and saucer, rinsing them out and leaving them in the otherwise empty sink. Then he returned to kiss her goodbye. "Don't get up. I'll let myself out." He hugged her.

"You take care, and promise me you'll call me and let me know how things go with your young man." She chuckled softly in his ear, and Chris released her. He closed the door behind him before making the short drive home, his mind whirring in myriad directions.

"CHRIS," PAVLE said as he came inside, with Briggs following behind him.

"How did it go?" Chris hurried in from the living room where he'd been watching television, meeting them in the kitchen. Well, he'd had it on, but found it hard to concentrate.

"He was amazing," Briggs said. "He identified our suspect without a moment's hesitation, and he provided some intimate details about him that will prove damaging, especially since knowing them proves the type of relationship they had." Briggs set his hat on the kitchen table, his equipment squeaking a little as he moved.

"Are you hungry?" Chris asked Pavle, who nodded and sat down quietly, his hands folded, resting on the table. Chris got to work making lunch. "Can you stay?" Chris asked Briggs.

"No. I need to get back. I talked to Marie this morning, and I was hopeful we had found the leak, but now I don't think so. Each of the people I suspected only viewed what they were supposed to. There was nothing out of the ordinary. Their access was granted specifically, and there was no way they could have gotten to anyone else's records." Briggs growled under his breath. "It's back to the drawing board."

"Maybe."

"I'm looking into other ways they could have gotten the information, but I don't see it. The leak has to be there somewhere. I made contact in Carlisle as well, and they are reviewing their records, but so far they have come up with nothing." Briggs picked up his hat. "We will find out who the traitor in our midst is, and so help me...."

"I know you will." Chris didn't want to say something silly, but Briggs was his hero. He was a good officer who knew how to do his job and did it well. In his time as interim sheriff, he had earned the respect of the men under him quickly.

"You keep him safe. Pavle is going to be an amazing witness once we bring this scum to trial." Briggs set his jaw, and Chris motioned toward the back door. He walked Briggs out through the yard. "This whole thing has everyone in the county up in arms. It's hit the papers and all the local news stations. The sheriff is getting nervous because he thought that once we caught this guy, the pressure would ease. But it isn't. Everyone wants to know who brought Pavle here. Pavle isn't the first person we've rescued this way in the last year. Though the other cases were women—which, don't get me wrong, still sucks—but none of them has gotten the media attention the way Pavle's has." Briggs clapped him on the shoulder. "I need you to keep him safe at all costs. The FBI sent over copies of the pictures he drew, and everyone who came in contact with him has a reason to be scared shitless." He plopped his hat on his head.

"I was there when he talked to them." Chris tried not to think about that too much. "It was upsetting. Some of it nearly made me sick." He coughed to cover his discomfort. "Has bail been set?"

"Yes. It was two million. He isn't going anywhere." Briggs actually smiled.

That was a relief. It meant Pavle was at least a modicum safer.

Briggs turned toward the back gate and then paused. "You call me if you see or hear anything out of the ordinary. I got the sheriff to increase patrols in this area of town under the guise of additional drug activity, and the local police are doing the same. There should always be someone no more than a few minutes away at any time. So don't hesitate to call for any reason." He pulled open the door and left the yard.

Chris locked all the doors behind him, then went back to making lunch.

"How many times I do this?" Pavle asked.

"A lot," Chris said, feeling for him. It was hell trying to get past something when the police, prosecutors, and social workers asked him about it every damn day. "I wish I could take it away, but I can't." He set the loaf of bread aside. "I know it's hard, but you're helping all of us and yourself. Anthony is behind bars, and it's doubtful he's going to get out. His bail is huge, and he doesn't have that kind of money."

"Good. He no hurt me anymore." The confidence in Pavle's voice was more than a little heartening. He really did have steel in his spine.

"That's right." There were other people who could hurt him, though, who were still out there. But one danger had been neutralized, and that was progress. Chris pulled out the chair and sat down next to Pavle. "Are you okay? What happened?" He had to know.

"Mr. Briggs nice to me. He take me to station, give me awful coffee." Pavle made a face. Chris knew exactly how bad that coffee was, especially by midmorning, after it had been sitting around getting stronger for hours. "Then he take me to room." Pavle tensed. "I scared INS come take me."

"Is that what he told you? Harvey Anthony?" Chris asked, and Pavle nodded.

"He say lots of things. That I bad, that they take me and hurt me. That if they come, they kill me and hide me. No one find me." Pavle sniffed. "I know he lie. I learn and smart. He nasty and stupid. But I scared." He sighed. "Briggs nice. He say I okay and show me pictures. I point out Anthony and tell him about ding-dong." Pavle turned away. "Tell him everything. Then he take me to other room. I shake head. He no right man. I tell Briggs and feel bad. But he nod."

*The decoy*, Chris realized. Briggs had to make sure Pavle wasn't going to finger just anyone.

"He take me to other room where he sit at table. He take me out to lobby. I happy when outside again. Then Briggs bring me here." Pavle shook. "I no want go back there."

"You aren't." That Chris could promise him without any doubt. "He's going to stay where he was."

The chime of the doorbell interrupted him. Chris squeezed Pavle's upper arm and left the table. When he reached the door, he peered through the window. Marie stood on the stoop, nervously shifting her weight. Chris opened the door.

"I heard that Pavle was at the police station this morning. Is he okay?"

"Yes." Chris motioned her inside. "Briggs was gentle with him. But the situation has upset him some. I'm about to make lunch. Come on in. You can talk with him. Friendly faces are what he needs." He smiled and led her through the house. Marie dropped her bag next to the table, and Pavle stood as she entered the room.

"I okay," Pavle told her. "I talk to Chris. He help me."

"Yes. That's good." She sat in the chair Chris had vacated. "There are going to be plenty of times when you have to tell what happened."

Pavle nodded. "Chris tell me."

Chris noticed that Pavle's gaze followed him as he moved through the room. He felt it almost as a touch.

"That's good. I've been thinking that at some point, Pavle might want to apply for asylum here." She reached into her bag and pulled out some forms. "You will need to decide if you want to stay or if you wish to go home."

"This home," Pavle said with a grin. "I stay with Chris."

Marie sighed. "Sweetheart, I mean, do you want to go back to Serbia? You were brought here, but illegally, so you can't stay unless we go through a process."

"Then I stay with Chris?" Pavle pressed.

"Pavle, Chris is protecting you so you can tell what happened to you to the police and in court. Once you do that, and if we can get an asylum hearing, then I will work with you to get a home of your own. That's what these papers are for."

As Chris placed a plate of cheese and crackers on the table, Pavle's expression fell like a collapsing soufflé. Chris glanced over the papers. "But he doesn't have a lot of this information. How can we fill this out?"

"I know." Marie turned to him. "You need to get it from the man in custody. If those items still exist, then he might have them. Those papers are part of what gets traded at ownership… usually. He's not going to give them up easily, but if Pavle wants to have any hope of an asylum hearing and staying in this country, then we need to find that information." She picked up a cracker but didn't eat it. "It can be done without them, but it's a hell of a lot harder and with a lot more risks."

"I'll tell Briggs. He can try to put some pressure on him."

"The most likely place would be a safe-deposit box. Those papers are treated like gold. With them he could trade and sell Pavle, control him. They are leverage against his behavior."

"Don't talk like I no here," Pavle said softly, his voice wavering.

"I'm sorry, that was rude of me. We need to find your papers. That will help a lot. Chris is going to see if he can help. We both will."

"I want stay with Chris." Pavle got up from the table and left the room.

Chris followed him with his eyes and then turned back to Marie. "I'll see what I can do."

She nodded slowly. "I'm concerned. Pavle is getting very emotionally involved with you. It happens sometimes."

"Of course he is. Pavle is a kind man, and I like him and care for him. He's been through hell and come out the other side." He hoped Marie didn't think she needed to pull Pavle away. He leaned closer. "Is it so bad that he's attached to me? There are worse people he could bond with."

"Of course there are," she said gently. "But how does he know what he really wants?" She took a bite of cracker and chewed. "Can you imagine going through what he did and then having someone like you being kind and gentle with him? He trusts you, and it's only natural that he might develop feelings for you." She finished the cracker, opened her bag, and pulled out a notebook. "Is he even gay?"

Chris nodded and looked toward the other room. "That's part of his shame and why he was leaving Serbia, at least in part."

Her lipstick-pink lips parted and her eyes widened. "I see. Give him some time to work things through and talk to him. Encourage him to talk with his therapist about this." She smiled. "I just want Pavle to be free to make his own decisions."

"That's what I want too."

She seemed to relax a little and stood. "I'm going to leave these forms for you. Fill in as much as you can, and hopefully we can locate Pavle's documents. Even if they're expired, it will help a great deal in authenticating who he says he is."

Chris walked her out and closed and locked the door. He went upstairs and found Pavle in the third bedroom that he used as a sitting room, curled up in the easy chair, gazing out the upper window that over-looked the street.

Pavle glanced at Chris as he entered the room. "I no want go somewhere else. I want stay here. I want this be my home." He turned back to the window. "I cannot go back to Serbia. I never able go home. There I shame… always shame."

"Then we'll make sure you don't have to go back. I'll help you."

Pavle turned toward him, looking more lost than he had when he'd first arrived. "I want to be here. I want stay with you and Nanna if I can." He sighed, sadness in his eyes. "I know too much to ask. Marie right. I need to go."

"I never said you had to go. I like having you here. We cook and garden, and we have fun." The fact that he'd had trouble sleeping ever since Pavle kissed him didn't enter into it at all.

"She say I go. Marie said. I hear. I want stay. I stay with you?" He seemed too hopeful.

"Yes. You can stay. She is worried about what you might be feeling. That you are getting close to me." Chris pulled up the other chair, ruffling the rug as he did. He sat down close enough that he could touch Pavle's hands. "She's afraid… and so am I… that you are developing feelings for me." He was doing this all wrong, he just knew it.

"What that mean?"

Chris had hoped he could beat around the bush a little, but that wasn't going to work. He laid it on the line. "She thinks you are falling in love with me and that I am falling in love with you."

"That bad?" Pavle asked. "I thought there no shame here."

"No. It's not bad. Falling in love is wonderful and happy." Chris smiled. "But I'm worried that, well, you've been through a lot."

"You think I stupid?" Pavle glared accusingly at Chris.

"No. But I want you to know how you feel." He waited and hoped. "Do you want to tell me?"

Pavle nodded. "I no have words." He lowered his gaze. "I want kiss you, hold you. I want spend night in same bed. No because you tell me. I want to. You make me safe and strong. I want to live with you and this be my home. Is that love?" He looked up at him.

The truth was, it sure sounded like it to Chris. "What does your heart tell you? Close your eyes and don't think. Just listen deep down and see what it says." Chris did the same, almost afraid to open his eyes as peace and calm descended over him. He breathed deeply, letting his head and the whirl of confusion around what he should do simply fade away, like a tornado that had blown itself out.

Slowly Chris opened his eyes to find Pavle leaning forward, looking at him hard enough that Chris could nearly feel it. "My heart say it want you." Pavle closed the distance between them. Their lips touched gently, a simple caress they deepened slowly, growing in intensity. Pavle leaned closer, adding more pressure, winding his hand around the back of Chris's neck.

Chris returned the kiss, his own heart fluttering with joy. But his head, well, that was another matter. The damn thing would not shut up. He gently placed his hands on Pavle's cheeks, stilling him. "Are you sure this is what you want?"

"You no want?" Pavle asked.

"I didn't say that. What I want isn't the issue." Chris placed his hands on top of Pavle's, smoothing them back to his side. "I was in love before. It was a while ago when I was in college." Chris entwined Pavle's fingers with his. "I was so in love with Louis. He was cute and smart, funny because he had no sense of humor at all. He thought he was funny, but he wasn't. Which was sort of funny in itself." He knew he'd lost Pavle by his rather blank gaze. "I fell in love with him, and I thought he and I were going to be together forever."

"But you no?" Pavle asked.

"No. He got a scholarship to another school and left. He went home for the summer, and we had plans to see each other, but then everything changed and he was gone." Chris cleared his throat. "I thought losing him was the end of the world, but then I learned he was my first love. Both of us were so young. Louis and I had our whole lives ahead of us, and we didn't know how much both of us were going to change in a short time."

Pavle narrowed his gaze. "What you mean?"

"A lot of things are changing for you, and they will continue to change. And what you want today might not be what you want in a month or three months." Chris gently squeezed Pavle's fingers. "I'm saying that I think I love you, but that I love you enough not to hold you too tight. You should be able to experience some life and happiness before you make up your mind. See, when I fall in love, for real, I want it to be forever."

"You no fall in love with Louis?" Pavle sat back a little in the chair.

"I don't know now," Chris answered. At the time, he'd thought he loved him, or he might have loved the feeling of being in love. Looking back, it was hard to know for sure.

"He hurt you?" Pavle's gaze hardened. "He here? In city? I rip face off for you."

Chris was speechless. His lips moved, but no words came out. "No," he said, then cleared his throat to get it working again. "Louis is far away."

"Good, then face safe." Pavle crossed his arms over his chest. Damn, he was cute when he was pissed off on Chris's behalf. "I want love too. Longtime love like Nanna. She say her and Poppy have wild... monkey... love. Whatever that is." For a second, after Chris stopped swallowing his tongue, he wondered just how much Pavle and Nanna had talked about. Or maybe he needed to rethink Nanna and Pavle spending so much time together. Nanna told tales, and Pavle certainly didn't need to know about his grandparents and anything involving monkeys in any way. "Nanna get weird look on face when she talk about him, like this." Pavle leaned back, looking like he was completely relaxed and about to light up a cigarette.

Chris coughed and had to catch his breath. "Good God, please." He needed eye bleach.

"I want look like that too."

Didn't everyone? Lord, Pavle and Nanna had had the talk about the birds and the bees and then skipped right to what made one's eyes roll to the back of their head.

"Okay. That's enough. I get the idea."

"No. I want make you look like that." Pavle still sat with his arms over his chest, leaning forward. "That what I want."

Jesus, Nanna and Marie had said to listen to what Pavle told him he wanted, but holy cow, he didn't expect Pavle to put things so eloquently, or graphically. Chris fanned himself with his hand as sweat broke out on his forehead. "How about you and I take things carefully?" One thing was for fucking sure, he was going to have to turn in his stud card if he wasn't careful. "You say you know what you want, and, well… I want to make sure that we don't regret things… so how about we learn about each other and see where things go?"

Pavle shook his head and then shrugged. "Sometimes you talk way too fucking much." He kissed Chris again and then backed away. "Did I say right?" He smiled, and all Chris could do was nod.

Yeah, Pavle had it about right. Sometimes talk was just overrated.

# CHAPTER 7

"I GET it," Pavle said when the doorbell rang.

"Okay, just be careful," Chris cautioned from the kitchen. He'd been doing a lot more cooking lately and found he didn't mind spending so much time in the kitchen. Chris turned down the heat under the pot of hamburger-vegetable soup to let it simmer and followed Pavle's path through the house.

"Reverend," Chris said as Pavle was about to close the door on the people he didn't know. "Please come in."

"Tyrone, please," the reverend said with a smile. "And you must be Pavle." He didn't seem upset that Pavle had nearly slammed the door on him. "This is Anika, my wife, and our son, Isaac."

Chris knew the instant Pavle recognized the toddler.

"You… you save me." Pavle smiled and sank back onto the bench Chris kept in the entryway.

"I'd say you saved yourself," Anika said. "I found your note when I was getting Isaac up one morning."

"I know… I no write good." Pavle bit his lower lip as Chris offered him a hand for support.

"Your note was fine. We knew you needed help and called the police. They found you and saved you." She offered Pavle a hand, and he released Chris's to take hers. "Tyrone and I want to help others. It's why he became a pastor and partly why I married him. A life of service is what we chose, but it's so rare to see the help we give someone pay off so quickly."

"I thank you for help," Pavle said formally. "I there long time."

"We had no idea. I was just assigned to rebuild this congregation a few months ago," Tyrone said.

Chris motioned them toward the living room. "Please come in." They took seats, with Pavle next to Anika, who still held his hand. He was so pleased Pavle wasn't scared of them and accepted the comfort and care they exuded from every pore. Chris left the room to set up a tray of lemonade and cheese and crackers in the kitchen. He brought it in as Pavle told his story, or at least an abbreviated version.

"I open window, throw note, close again. Then pray," Pavle was saying as he returned and put the tray on the coffee table. "People no know there more like me here. They need help, but hard to find."

"Yes, they are. And the neighborhood near our church is a good place to hide." Reverend Tyrone took a glass of lemonade and handed it to Anika. "I want to work to help build a sense of community around us." He looked over at Chris. "Do you have any suggestions to help us get started? Since you've been here longer than we have, that would be helpful."

"Have you contacted the garden people?" Chris asked.

"Not yet."

"They are the ones who built and maintain the gardens and trees in the park area. I bet they would be willing to help you. They love that neighborhood and would probably work with you to spearhead your cleanup campaign. The leader is Marilyn Smith. I can get her number for you. I'm sure they would appreciate your help."

Tyrone nodded enthusiastically. "Common goals. I love that."

"Yes, and I can put you in touch with Red. He was the police officer with me when we visited. I'll help too. We are all interested in cleaning up neighborhoods. The stronger the community, the less crime and issues we all have."

Tyrone smiled brightly. "I wasn't expecting so much support. It seemed like a daunting task."

"I help too," Pavle offered.

"Excellent," Tyrone said. He turned to Pavle. "They are going to tear down the house next to ours."

"Has the church contacted the borough? They could donate it to the church or sell it to you. Then you would have control over it."

"I hadn't thought of that. I thought it was owned by someone."

"It was, but they probably signed it over to the borough so they don't have to incur the direct costs of tearing it down and cleaning up the mess. They would have had to if things are moving that quickly with re-moving it."

"We could add the lot to the community garden space… or build one of our own for our parishioners." Tyrone seemed to have plenty of ideas.

"I wanted to invite you to come to church with us on Sunday," Anika said quietly, during a break in Chris's conversation with Tyrone.

"That very nice," Pavle said. "I no go out much. Men trying to hurt me. They scared because I know them."

Both Anika and Tyrone turned to Chris, probably for an explanation, who in turn looked at Pavle. He seemed to be struggling for words. "Will you tell?" Pavle asked.

"He's been able to describe all the people he's come in contact with, and it seems they are tracking him down. So we don't get out much, for his protection. I think it would be good for him. Pavle, if you want to go, I will take you."

"Will they like me?" Pavle turned to Chris, eyes filled with doubt and, damn it all, shame. Chris could see the insecurity rising inside him.

"Of course we will," Reverend Tyrone said. "Our church is inclusive, and we believe that all people have a right to dignity and love." He reached out to Pavle. "It is my belief that God made man in his own image and that God is perfect. But the rest of us, we need support and his love to overcome what life throws at us. So yes, you will be welcome and your life celebrated, just like those of everyone else." He turned to Chris. "We are Methodists, and views differ widely, but that is what I believe and what I teach."

"Then I come." Pavle smiled and leaned in to Isaac, who grinned when Pavle tickled him a little. "You a happy small man." Pavle tickled him again, and Isaac slid off his mother's lap and onto the sofa, then climbed onto Pavle. He plopped himself down, grinning up at Pavle as though he hung the moon. Pavle smiled as Isaac giggled louder.

"He likes tickles," Anika said.

"He good boy," Pavle said, and turned to Chris. "You got toys?"

Chris wasn't sure what he had, but he checked the closet in the back room and found a box of large-size

Legos from when he was a kid. He brought them to the living room and handed Pavle the blue cloth bag. Pavle and Isaac slid onto the floor, and Pavle emptied the blocks on the rug. He didn't seem to know what to do with them, but once he figured it out, he and Isaac built a tower, which Isaac knocked down, to giggles and laughs.

Chris watched Pavle, who smiled and laughed when Isaac laughed. "That's so good to hear."

"What?" Anika asked quietly.

"Him laughing." Chris realized it was the first time he'd heard it. He slid off onto the floor to join them. "What time are services?"

"Ten thirty on Sunday," Tyrone said. "Both of you will be very welcome."

"That's great. Pavle needs places where he can feel welcome and part of a community."

Isaac knocked down yet another tower. It crashed to pieces, sending blocks everywhere. Isaac put his hands over his head in a show of joy, laughing happily.

"We have some parishioners to visit," Tyrone said after a few more towers had been built and demolished.

"Isaac, help Mr. Pavle pick up all the blocks," Anika said, and Isaac scrambled around the room, putting the blocks back in the bag.

Once they were all picked up, Pavle closed the bag and set it on the table, took Isaac's hand, and led him to the door. "Thank you helping me." He hugged both Anika and Tyrone. "You save me."

"You're welcome, honey. We were glad it worked out, and it's nice to meet you." She stepped back. "We'll see you on Sunday." She and Tyrone shook Chris's hand, and then he saw them out and closed the door.

"They nice." Pavle slipped his arms around Chris's waist, leaning against his back, sending heat running through him. "I lucky."

Chris wasn't a religious man. He never had been. "Sometimes prayers are answered." He could imagine Tyrone saying that, and Chris knew in his heart it was true. If any prayer needed to be answered, it had been Pavle's. Chris tried not to think about Pavle scratching out an existence in that small, airless room. It made his blood boil each time he did it. "But you were the one who helped yourself." Chris turned around. "Don't forget that."

Pavle squeezed a little closer. "I no forget. But I lucky. They nice and help me."

"Yes."

"And they black."

Chris frowned. "What does that matter?"

"It no to me. But Master Anthony, he no like them, call them names. So when I see Isaac, I think if he hate, then maybe they really nice. Master Anthony was…."

"A real jackass," Chris finished.

"Yes. That," Pavle agreed. "He no nice to anyone." Pavle shivered, and Chris nodded. "I no like him at all. He hate lots of people, and…."

A clearer picture of this man was starting to form in Chris's mind. "He took out his frustrations with people he hated on you?"

Pavle nodded slowly and swallowed. "He hurt me. When he angry, it get bad." Pavle stepped back, rubbing his upper left arm. "Sometimes he hurt bad. I feel sick and he no feed me for long time." Pavle lowered his gaze. "I beg for food. He like that."

Chris pulled Pavle to him, holding him tightly. "He was a sick man." Damn it all. He'd heard those kinds of stories before. No one should ever have to go through something like that. And knowing that Pavle had went right to his heart and made it ache on his behalf. "But he's gone now."

"I know. No at night, sometimes. I see him when I sleep. He come for me, and I wake up." Pavle sighed. "I hate it. Want him go away forever and always."

"That will happen with time. You just keep being strong. He will go to jail, where bad things happen to people like him. He isn't going to be able to hurt you anymore, and the last time you see him will be when you tell what happened to you in court."

"I have to see him?" Pavle shook.

"Yes, unless he pleads guilty." That wasn't likely to happen. Not with someone like him. These men thought themselves above the law and all human decency. Everything they did was someone else's fault, and they compartmentalized everything to the point that they didn't see anything they did as wrong.

"You safe me?" Pavle asked.

"Yes. I'll do everything I can to protect you." Chris released Pavle. "I have to make a few phone calls. Is that okay?" Pavle nodded, and Chris checked his watch once Pavle went into the other room.

Chris went through the house to the back sitting room and called Briggs. "Any luck getting Pavle's papers?" he asked once Briggs answered.

"No. He's refusing to talk to anyone other than his lawyer, and he isn't going to give that up. If he does, it's an admission of guilt."

"Can we subpoena his safe-deposit boxes?" Chris asked.

"We did and came up empty as far as the papers were concerned. He might have another somewhere, but it's hard to check every single bank in town. I have a deputy working that angle, but it's a long shot."

"Do we need to pressure him?" Chris asked. "Get him to do the right thing whether he wants to or not?" He wasn't above playing some mind games in order to get what Pavle needed.

"The last time we put him in a room to question him, all he said was he wanted his lawyer and then refused to say anything, even with the lawyer present... not a single word. I don't know what leverage we can get to make him talk." Briggs seemed as frustrated as Chris had ever heard him.

"You're probably right. We need to think about it. Maybe listen at the jail, see if anyone heard anything that might give us an insight. Prisoners talk all the damn time."

Briggs sighed. "Kid, this guy is like a steel trap. He doesn't talk to anybody. I'll keep working on it, but I'm not particularly hopeful." He cleared his throat. "Has there been anything unusual on your end?"

"No. It's quiet, almost too quiet. Do you think they've gone to ground?" Chris asked.

"Not on your life. These are people who will stop at nothing to get what they want. I suspect they are looking harder, and whoever their contact is has got to be pretty damn stressed because they're probably pressuring him for information. Just stay away and out of sight. Apparently your mother has taken a turn for the worse and is fighting cancer while your dad has been having health issues, so you're needed there, and the sheriff has granted you extended leave. If anyone asks, I've told people that I'm watching your house for you. Keep the curtains in front pulled and the garage doors locked and closed. The last thing we want is for them to get wind that you're in town."

"But I had visitors today." Chris swallowed, realizing he might have screwed up royally. "The minister and his family... the ones who found Pavle's note, as well as Marie."

"Shit...." Briggs swore under his breath. "Don't have any more, and come and go as unobtrusively as possible. Various group homes and safe houses have reported people watching them. They are all jumpier than cats, and we don't have any proof, but someone is keeping up the interest. The FBI has put out calls using Pavle's drawings, so pressure is mounting. If we want to get these men, then we have to keep Pavle safe."

"Should we leave town?"

Briggs paused. "I thought of that, but if you did, you'd have less protection. The police and sheriff's department are available to back you up here. If you left, you'd be on your own. Just stay put and keep out of sight."

"Okay." Chris blew out a breath of frustration. "Pavle wants to go to church on Sunday. They invited him, and he really wants to go." It was going to be hard for Chris to tell him no.

"Hell."

"I know. But I can't keep him locked up here. He needs to be out sometimes. After all, he isn't a criminal."

"True. But if they find him, he... and you could end up dead. I'm not going to tell you not to, but be damned careful and try not to let people see you come and go. Also be watchful. For now, from the indications we're getting, no one seems to have made the connection between you and Pavle, but I don't know how much longer that's going to last."

Chris sighed. "Okay. I'll be careful." He checked that there was nothing else Briggs needed and ended the call. He sat in his chair, looking out over the back-yard, keeping the lights off inside and wondering what he was going to do. It was just a matter of time before someone figured out where Pavle was. His hope was that the FBI was able to find the people Pavle had iden-tified before they found him.

"Chris," Pavle said as he came in, interrupting his worried thoughts. "I no watch alone."

"It's okay." Chris held out his hand, and Pavle took it, sliding his fingers over Chris's. "I don't like to watch television alone either."

Pavle sat on the arm of Chris's chair. "Who you talk to?"

"Briggs. He's trying to find your papers, but An-thony isn't talking to anyone. We think he might have them, and we need them so we can help you stay in this country."

"He nasty man. Want something. Never give any-thing to anyone." Pavle leaned closer, and Chris closed his eyes as he wrapped his arms around him. Pavle had made clear what he wanted, and holding him seemed as natural for Chris as breathing. Part of him said to just give in and take Pavle upstairs to show him how won-derful things could be between two people who cared for each other. And yet, he wasn't able to. As much as he wanted to, it had to be Pavle who made that decision.

"We are working on how we can get him to change his mind." Chris wondered if Marie might have some suggestions. She really seemed to understand how a man like that thought and would react, since she'd dealt with their victims. Her insight might be helpful. "Why don't you and I go into the kitchen and make something for dinner. I have some chicken wings, or we can have the soup we made." He smiled. "Do you like spicy food?"

Pavle nodded. "Mama liked spice."

Then buffalo wings it was. He could bake them, and he had some sauce he could heat up to put on them. "I do too. So I'll make us some spicy chicken, and you can help if you want."

Chris leaned forward to get up, but Pavle didn't release him, getting closer. "We cook later." He held Chris tighter, so Chris sat still. This was too nice to rush, warm and gentle, even if his heart raced at lightning speed. He breathed deeply, enjoying a quiet moment together.

CHRIS SAID good night to Pavle and went to the bathroom, where he took a shower and pulled on a pair of sleep shorts and T-shirt for bed. He crossed the hall to his room, glancing at the closed door to Pavle's, licking his lips. Pavle had kissed him again while they'd sat in the chair. Chris had been kissed before… and done a lot more, so what made that one different? He wanted to talk to someone, but the only person he could think of was Nanna, and he refused to ask his grandmother about kissing a boy. Though apparently Nanna was some kind of expert.

He closed the door and slipped under the covers, turning out the light. After lying still for ten minutes, he pushed back the covers and left the room with a sigh, going back downstairs to check that he'd locked all the doors and to peer out of the front curtains just to make sure nothing out of the ordinary was going on. Parked cars lined the street and a vehicle drove past, but there were no shadowy figures waiting in trench coats like in the movies. The conversation with Briggs had Chris's imagination running on overtime. He left a small light burning in the living room and turned out the light on the stairs once he'd reached the top, then went to his room and got back into bed.

He lay awake on his back, staring up at the ceiling, his head and heart racing a mile a minute. He was nervous, and every sound in the old house left him on edge. Chris sat up at a creak in the hallway, listening for more, but heard nothing. Now he knew he was imagining things. Still, he got up to check as his door opened. Chris braced himself, arms up, legs apart, ready for a fight, as Pavle stepped into his room.

"What you doing?" Pavle asked when he saw what must have been him looking like one of the guys who gets kicked in the gut and goes down easy in a kung fu movie.

"I could ask you the same thing." Chris stared at Pavle, who was wearing his old plaid pajamas that were a size too big for him. He relaxed as Pavle put his hands on his hips, gaze raking over Chris with enough intensity to raise the temperature in the room ten degrees. "Was there something you needed?"

Pavle's hands slipped to his sides and his stance lightened. "I…." He turned, looking at the bed.

"Is something wrong?" Chris walked around the far side of the bed and sat down. "What happened?"

Pavle's gaze traveled to him and then over the bed. He shifted his weight slightly and then seemed to make up his mind. Pavle approached the bed, pulled down the covers, and slipped between them. He tugged them up, leaning against the headboard.

"Pavle…," Chris whispered. Damn, he looked good in Chris's bed.

"This what I want," Pavle said quietly, and Chris swallowed. "I lay over there and no want to be there. I want you, but no know how to say and you no understand." He bit his lower lip. "I tell you, but you no listen. So I show." Pavle's right arm shook a little, and Chris realized just how afraid Pavle was that he was going to be rejected.

"I know. And I know what I want too." Chris leaned over the bed to gently kiss Pavle, who pulled him in, intensifying the kiss until Chris thought the top of his head would blow off. To be wanted and desired that way was nearly too much. Chris backed away, looking into Pavle's eyes. "I need you to tell me. Is this what you really want? You know you do not have to do this to stay here."

Pavle rolled his eyes like a teenager. "You already say." He crossed his arms over his chest. "You no want me?" he asked.

That had been what he was trying to avoid—that hurt look. God, Chris did want him. Pavle was adorable, and whether Chris liked it or not, Pavle already held Chris's heart in his hands. He hadn't meant to give it to him; it had just happened.

"I do," he admitted out loud. "I really do. But I don't want you to—"

There was that expression again. "I no baby. I know own head." He pointed and patted the bed next to him. Chris climbed under the covers, lying down as he watched Pavle, who grinned and shimmied farther under the covers, pulling close to him.

"Will you sleep better now?" Chris asked, because he sure as hell wasn't likely to fall to sleep any time soon, not with Pavle's intense heat so near.

"I sleep good now." Pavle kissed him on the cheek, his hands sliding across Chris's belly, and then he pressed right against him. "We go slow, like you say."

Chris swallowed hard and nodded. It seemed Pavle was taking things into his own hands. He knew that's how things had to be, but with his body on overdrive and Pavle, the heat furnace, right next to him, there was no way he was going to be able to go to sleep. "Okay. We can go slow."

"But no too slow," Pavle said.

"What does that mean?" Chris asked, amused. "Why don't you tell me what you want?"

"I want to sleep here. I want us to take off clothes and be together. But you not ready for that." Pavle scooted around, getting comfortable.

Chris opened his mouth to argue, but snapped it shut again. He hadn't wanted to think of it that way, but maybe Pavle was right. He wasn't ready to jump into a physical relationship with Pavle. Not because he didn't want to, but because he was worried about…. Jesus, he was doing it again, making decisions about Pavle when Pavle was capable of making them himself. "I'm not?"

"No. You scared," Pavle pronounced as though he had all the answers. Maybe he did. Arguing with him wasn't going to get Chris anywhere, especially not when Pavle looked at him with those big brown eyes and lips set firmly. "I know what like to be fear. I know… I do." Pavle patted Chris's chest. "You scared here and need to know what want." He patted Chris once again, right over his heart. "You no need be scared. I not feary." He sat up and leaned to kiss Chris softly. "Good night." He lay back down and closed his eyes.

Sometimes Chris wondered if he was ever going to understand Pavle, but maybe he should be more concerned that Pavle seemed to understand him all too well. Granted, Chris wasn't scared, but cautious, especially where Pavle was concerned. If this had been any other man, he would have probably taken him to bed and made passionate love to him some time ago. He'd also know that he understood the ramifications of what they did together. He wasn't sure of that with Pavle. That concerned him and held him back.

"Good night," he told Pavle, and slipped under the covers, rolling onto his side and closing his eyes as he slid one arm under his pillow.

Pavle lay still and then rolled over as well, pressing to Chris and skidding his arm around his waist. In the near silence, Pavle sighed and seemed to relax next to him, like he felt this was right. Chris could only hope that was true, even as he stared into the darkness toward the bedroom door.


A CRASH had Chris bolting upright. He listened and barely heard whispering coming in through the open window.

"Get this out of here and be quiet. He's a cop and something is going on over there."

Chris slipped out of bed without turning on the light. Pavle woke briefly and then rolled over once Chris moved away. He took a second to look at him before padding out of the room and over to the window of the landing, which overlooked the neighbor's yard.

Two men carried boxes out of the house and toward the garage, returning a few minutes later for more. "I told you this was a bad place to set up shop." They stopped, setting the boxes on the sidewalk, and returned inside.

Chris went back to his room and got his phone off the nightstand, then went to the bathroom because the windows weren't open in there. "Briggs, it's Chris. I know I can't call this in, but my neighbor to the east is carrying boxes out to the garage at this time of night. I heard him say to be quiet and that I was a cop. One of the other men said that it was a terrible idea to set up shop here."

"Have you ever noticed anything?"

"Other than the guy is paranoid and a little weird, no. I know this isn't much to go on." Chris wished he knew what was in those boxes. Knowing in his gut that something was wrong and being able to prove it were two different things. The police would respond to a citizen call like that, but as an officer, he was held to a higher standard.

He left the bathroom and returned to the landing window as they came out again. One of the men tripped over something, the box he was carrying flipping down the sidewalk. It wasn't light enough for Chris to see much clearly, but the contents seemed to have spilled out on the walk.

"It's pot," he whispered to Briggs as the cloyingly sweet scent reached his nose.

"Sweep that up fast," someone said. "And get it out of here right now." The voice was getting desperate.

"I'll call the Carlisle PD. You stay inside and keep Pavle away. Pretend you're not home unless they specifically knock on your door. I'll meet them there." Briggs hung up, and Chris stood far enough back that he couldn't be seen but could still see what was going on.

Minutes later, lights flashed outside, and then there was the dull thud of a door being kicked in and officers swarmed out of the house and garage into the backyard.

His neighbor and another man fell to the ground as po-lice covered the area, taking them into custody.

Chris went back to his room, where Pavle stood looking out the window, shaking. Chris hoped this wasn't triggering a flashback.

"What happening?" Pavle asked as Chris ushered him back, holding him for a few seconds for reassur-ance. "I okay," he said breathily, and Chris got the idea that Pavle was trying to be strong and cover up at least some of his reaction, but the stress still carried through in Pavle's hold on him.

"They are arresting him for drugs, I think." Chris slowly closed the window. "Go on back to sleep. I need to make sure everything is safe and secure." Chris put on his robe and met Briggs at his back door, letting him and Red inside.

"Is everything under control?" Chris asked.

"Yes. Are you guys okay?" Red asked before Briggs could respond.

Chris nodded. "I smelled the drugs when one of the packages spilled open. They're really strong, judging by the scent."

"Well, there's even more in the basement. It seems there was a regular distribution center going on. It looks like it was mainly out of the garage and they moved large quantities. The basement is specially ventilated up through one of the chimneys, so any scent was kept away from ground level. I think it was a newer opera-tion, but they must have gotten scared and decided to move on," Red explained, looking out the back.

"I had a talk with my relatively new neighbor a few days ago when he seemed curious about what was going on in my yard, and I told him he needed to mind his own business or I'd take an interest in his. I think that spooked him. He hasn't been living there long, and I don't think he realized I was a deputy until that day."

Briggs stepped forward. "What did he ask you?"

"He heard Pavle and started asking if he was Russian. It really upset Pavle, and pissed me off. So I poked my head over the fence and explained that I was a county deputy. I had no idea anything was actually going on over there. He kept to himself, and other than passing him on the sidewalk a few times, I never gave him a second thought. I had him over just after he moved in to be neighborly. Why?"

"Did he see Pavle?" Briggs asked.

"Not that I know of, though he must have heard us out in the yard. There isn't exactly privacy back here. The fence keeps him from looking in, but he can probably see from up there." Chris opened the back closet and extracted the files from his motion cameras. "I don't know how much of his yard is going to be visible, but these are the tapes of the back. It's dark, and I don't know what there is on it, but you're welcome to it." Briggs passed it to Red, who went out the back.

"You don't think he was interested in Pavle?" Briggs pressed.

"No. I think he heard him speaking another language and was curious. He peered over into the yard, but there was nothing in particular to see—I'd sent Pavle inside." Chris paused. "You don't think my neighbor…?"

"No. I don't. He's a dealer or working for an organization that we'll get to the bottom of, but I don't think he has anything to do with Pavle. But I want to be sure. There has been a lot of activity around him and you lately." Briggs clapped him on the shoulder. "You have to know that you're going to get some shit from the guys for having a drug house next to you and not knowing it."

"Yeah, I figured. Even if I was the one to finger them." Chris rolled his eyes.

"You were on the ball and that's good, but no one can know it was you who broke this up. You aren't in town. Just keep your head low and watch Pavle. Something is going to happen—I can feel it in my bones. They'll keep looking for him, and when they get one clue, all hell will break loose." Briggs wiped his eyes. "You get back to bed, and I'll come over to talk to both you and Pavle in the morning to see if there is anything more he can tell us. I also am expecting an update from our FBI friends, and I'll let you know what's happening on that front too." He said good night and left the house, going through the garden and then out the back gate, probably to join the others.

Chris locked up the house and checked the activity next door before returning to his room. Pavle was still awake when Chris got into bed.

"I scared," Pavle whispered.

"I know." Chris put an arm around Pavle and whispered for him to roll over. Then Chris gently rubbed his back until Pavle's breathing evened out and he fell to sleep. Chris, on the other hand, heard everything outside for hours and didn't get to sleep until the activity quieted down just before dawn.

BRIGGS SHOWED up just about the time Chris came down to make breakfast. He sipped his second cup of coffee, trying to wake up after just a few hours' sleep.

"We have a problem," Briggs said.

"What?"

"Well, the guy next door has been telling every-one that his neighbor is a deputy and that he had some-thing against him and that's why he arranged all this." Briggs sat down. "The sheriff knows you've been watching Pavle, but it's becoming clear that you're back in town, so he says you need to return to at least partial regular duty." Briggs was clearly as unhappy as Chris was.

"Where I go?" Pavle asked, holding Chris's arm.

"You—"

"Nanna's," Chris answered. "She needs some help during the day, and the two of you can keep each other company." Chris looked at Briggs, hoping he kept his mouth closed. He wasn't going to have Pavle shipped off to someone else and passed around like some hot potato.

Pavle grinned. "That good idea. She and I cook, and we talk." He practically bounced with excitement. Of course, Chris wondered just what the two of them would get up to, but what the heck.

"Your grandmother's?" Briggs asked.

"No one is going to look for him at her house, and she and Pavle get along. Also, she can get in touch with either of us on a moment's notice. I think it's important that Pavle not feel like he's being held prisoner again."

"But your grandmother?" Briggs asked, as skep-tical as Chris had ever seen him. "What is she going to do when people barge into her home? Talk them to death, make them cookies?"

Chris laughed, hard. "What she'll do is blow their brains out as soon as they come through the door. Nanna is a crack shot and spent thirty years shoot-ing competitively. You know—skeet, clay pigeons. Nanna can shoot one hundred out of one hundred, ten times in a row. A thousand dead-on shots. She and Poppy used to shoot together competitively. They used to have cases full of ribbons and trophies. She packed them up after Poppy died, but there's no one I'd trust Pavle with more."

Briggs's mouth hung open. "You have to be kidding. Shooting skeet is different from shooting a person."

"You don't know my nanna. She escaped from behind the iron curtain, with guts and determination. You think she'd let anything or anyone hurt her family? She considers Pavle family, and Pavle likes her and knows her." Chris could already feel Pavle's nails digging into his arm.

"You're serious?" Briggs said.

"Yes. We'll just need to make sure it's done in a way so he isn't seen." Chris sighed. "There's more to this than just safety. Pavle needs to be comfortable." He turned to Pavle.

Pavle nodded.

"I don't think—" Briggs stopped when he saw the wall of "no" in front of him.

Chris stepped closer to Briggs. "It's time someone asked Pavle what he wanted. It's his safety and his decision. So if he wants to go to Nanna's while I'm at work, then that's fine. She could use a little help, and they speak the same language. If you want to have someone stop by occasionally to check on them, you can, and I will call throughout the day. But I think he needs to be with someone he's comfortable with."

Pavle's grip on his arm lessened.

Briggs shook his head slowly. "I think you're crazy, but I can't force him to go where he doesn't want to."

"I stay with Nanna," Pavle said.

"I'll take him over on my way to work and pick him up after my shift." This whole thing was getting complicated, but Chris would do whatever was necessary to help keep Pavle safe.

"All right," Briggs said. "I'll ask Pierre to stop by on a regular basis to check on them, but I don't want a parade of people going in and out. That will only draw attention. Pavle, you need to stay at Nanna's and not go out."

"Not even in sun?" Pavle asked.

"Stay in the backyard," Chris clarified. "You can go outside, just don't leave the yard. This is to keep you safe. It shouldn't be a problem, because as long as they don't know where you are, you'll be just fine. Okay?"

Pavle digested the information and then agreed.

"This isn't ideal, but what choice do I have?" Briggs asked.

"Not much." Chris smiled, and Pavle let go of Chris and left the room. "Pavle was in a prison of someone else's making for years. You know that. We can't put him in another one, even for his safety."

Briggs didn't argue, but he did widen his eyes. "You really understand him."

Chris hmphed. "Sometimes I think I do, and then Pavle surprises me." He smiled. "He isn't helpless, Briggs. Pavle is strong and knows what he wants. It's taken me some time to realize that."

"But if anything happens to him…."

Chris was well aware of what would occur if anything were to happen to Pavle. It was likely their case would fall apart. But even more, it was doubtful Chris's heart would ever recover from the loss. "Then we need to make sure nothing does, and the best way to do that is by doing our jobs and finding whoever is behind this." Defense was only going to get them so far.

"I can't argue with your logic." Briggs stood and turned to leave. "I'll tell the sheriff that you'll be in tomorrow for your shift. See you then." Briggs exited the way he came, and Chris went to find Pavle.

"I really stay with Nanna?" Pavle asked.

"Only during the day. I'll pick you up on my way home from work, and you'll be here with me," Chris confirmed. "I'm not asking you to leave, and on Sunday I'll take you to church like I promised." Chris had no intention of letting Pavle go unless he asked to leave. That was a different matter, and if Pavle wanted to go, he was free to do so at any time. But until he asked, Chris would fight to protect him physically, as well as his right to make his own decisions.

"But for how long I stay with you?" Pavle asked.

"As long as you want." Chris would give Pavle a home. "And just so you know, that is not conditional on you sharing my bed… or anything else." He had to make that clear. "I love you, Pavle. I do." He couldn't stop the words from coming forward. "You have worked your way into my heart, and that's all there is to it. But I don't want you to think that you have to sleep with me or… well… anything else. I don't want you to think I'm like the men who hurt you."

Pavle rolled his eyes like he had the night before. "I no think that. You kind and strong. You good man— they not." He stepped closer and raised up on his toes to kiss him gently. "I love you too. I think."

"You think?" Chris chuckled because sometimes Pavle was too cute for words.

"I no know what love like. I love Mama and Papa, but I never know this kind of love." Pavle put his hand over Chris's heart.

Chris looked into Pavle's eyes without thinking about it. "You make me want to spend time with you and be with you." He swallowed. "You warm my heart and make my life a little brighter even on the coldest day."

Pavle's lips parted. "I do that?" he whispered.

"Yes. And loving someone means you want to protect and care for them for as long as they'll let you." Chris smoothed his hands over Pavle's stubble-rough cheeks. "At first I thought it was some police instinct to protect you, but it's more than that. So very much more."

Pavle blinked slowly. "You…." He turned to glance behind him. "This how feel for me?"

"Yes." A stab of worry raced through Chris. He'd spilled his guts, confessing how he felt, and Pavle didn't believe him. Or maybe he didn't feel the same way. Chris probably should have kept his mouth shut. He'd been worried about pushing Pavle, and maybe that's what he'd just done. It was too late to take anything back now that he'd laid it all out.

"Oh. That very nice." Pavle smiled. "I like you think that. Make me safe, I like that. I want this to be home, right here." He leaned closer. "I want you be home. Do I say right?" He grinned.

"You said it right. But why do you want this to be your home?" Chris asked.

"Because you here," Pavle answered, and Chris was more than happy with that. "You make happy and smile… much. I want help you too, make you smile."

"You already do that," Chris whispered, standing still, not wanting to move in case he broke the spell between them. Slowly Chris leaned forward, and Pavle did the same. Their arms slid around each other, and Pavle kissed him. This time it wasn't gentle, but harder, insistent. He moaned softly, and suddenly Chris was back in the interview room at the courthouse, those stories Pavle had told ringing in his head. He shivered and pushed the images and anger that threatened back down. He already knew how things were before, and this was nothing like that. Chris tenderly ran his fingers through Pavle's hair, stroking his scalp.

"Why you stop?" Pavle asked.

Chris blinked and realized he was just standing still. "I worry sometimes. That's why I have to go slow. I don't want you to think of me the way… like the others."

"You not. I not." Pavle stilled as well. "Do you think me… shame? That I no all together?" He blinked and bit his lower lip.

"No. I don't think you're broken. I think you're strong and that you didn't break. You never gave up." Chris clenched his lips as hurt and pain washed off Pavle and over Chris like a wave. For a second, he could feel everything that Pavle had gone through and survived. It was like something clicked inside his head and he understood. It was some kind of momentary spiritual connection. "You are not broken." Though if Chris were honest, he wondered if the same experience wouldn't have broken him.

Pavle smiled a little, releasing his tortured lip, and Chris kissed it, glossing his tongue along to soothe it before kissing him harder once again. Pavle pressed to him, wriggling and shifting his weight as though he couldn't get close enough.

"Sweetheart, are you sure?" Chris asked, and when Pavle nodded, Chris swept him off his feet and carried him through the house.

"Chris, I no baby," Pavle said through laughter. "You no caveman."

When Chris set Pavle on his feet, he hit the stairs and scampered up. Chris hurried after him, laughing too hard to really go very fast. It had been a long time since he'd actually laughed like this as a prelude to sex.

Chris stopped at the top of the stairs just outside his room as Pavle sprawled on the bed, bouncing. This was really going to happen, and he was laughing, smiling, and having an amazing time. Yeah, he should be doing all that, because there was sex in the future, but he'd always been nervous at this point in the process. He didn't feel that this time. There was only excitement and anticipation, making his blood race and his heart thump faster and faster.

"What taking so long?" Pavle sang out, and Chris hurried in.

Pavle grinned as he propped himself up on his elbows, watching every move Chris made as he gradually approached the bed. He had intended to go slowly and make sure Pavle was comfortable, but as he leaned over the bed, Pavle wound his arms around Chris's neck and drew him close.

"Are you sure about this?" Chris kept his voice serious. "I want you to be comfortable and happy."

"Then make with the happy," Pavle said, rolling his eyes. He was doing that a lot lately, and damned if it wasn't cute.

"Like this?" Chris asked, kissing Pavle gently and slipping his hands under his shirt to lift the fabric. He broke the kiss long enough to pull off Pavle's shirt before pressing him back on the bed. Chris paid close attention to Pavle's reaction, making sure he was comfortable. The last thing he wanted to do was remind Pavle in any way of… well, he didn't need to name him… not now. "Or like this…?" Chris sucked at the base of Pavle's neck, licking and caressing him just enough that Pavle shook under him.

"Chris…." Pavle held him tighter, quivering and shaking as Chris moved lower, closing his lips around a nipple and using his tongue to tweak the hard bud. "Oh…." He moaned softly and slapped his hand over his mouth.

"What's that for?" Chris gently took his hand and tugged it away. "You can make sounds. I prefer if you did—the louder and happier, the better." He smiled and nodded, holding Pavle's hand as he returned to the feast of skin and heat that was Pavle. He wanted to make him moan, groan, and whimper, loud and long.

"I no used to it."

Chris squeezed Pavle's hand. "I hope you get used to it. Because nothing would make me happier than for you to get used to being happy." He swirled his tongue in Pavle's belly button, the muscles fluttering as Pavle giggled. Then, as Chris ran his hand along the ridge under his jeans, the sound morphed into a quiet moan whose beauty rumbled in Pavle's throat. "You like that?"

"Yes…." Pavle gasped. Chris lifted his gaze to Pavle's glassy eyes as he held his breath and didn't move. "Chris…."

Chris unfastened the clasp on Pavle's jeans and parted the fabric to lick the trail of exposed skin, inhaling the deep richness of Pavle's scent as he buried his nose against him. "You're beautiful." He inhaled again, the aroma wrapping around the pleasure centers of his brain, taking root so he could always remember.

Pavle's cheeks reddened as Chris tugged the fabric lower and then off his legs. Chris stared at a naked and vulnerable Pavle, and his heart skipped a beat.

"I scared," Pavle whispered.

Chris backed away. "Why?"

"What if you no like me?" Pavle asked, and Chris's eyes widened. Pavle propped himself up on his elbows once again, even as Chris's mouth went dry and his eyes bugged out of his head.

"Not like you?" He gathered Pavle in his arms, holding him tightly. "You are amazingly beautiful and precious." That was the only word that came to mind. He cradled Pavle, kissing him, pouring everything he had into the touch between them. Pavle clung to him, holding and whimpering as Chris once again found that spot at the base of his neck. "Damn, you make me want you so badly." He pressed Pavle back on the bed, pausing to look into his eyes. "I will never hurt you," he promised.

"I know. But what if I no enough?"

Chris held Pavle tighter. "You are more than enough." He slid along Pavle's body, licking his way down his belly before sucking Pavle's length between his lips.

Pavle gasped and groaned as Chris took him deep, whimpered as Chris took all of him. Chris buried his nose against Pavle's skin, swirling his tongue and giving Pavle everything he had. Damn, Pavle tasted great, and his cock sliding over Chris's tongue was heaven. His own cock throbbed in his jeans, aching for attention. He managed to unfasten his pants without breaking his rhythm, driving a shaking Pavle to the highest heights of passion possible. At least he hoped so.

It took a few minutes, but Pavle finally let go, moaning more loudly and even bucking against him. That was what he wanted, for Pavle to release some of his reticence and let himself go in the moment. Chris knew that was going to be hard for him, and seeing and feeling it sent a whole new wave of heat rushing through him.

"Chris…." Pavle whimpered.

Chris sucked harder, taking all of Pavle's girth between his lips, hollowing out his cheeks while stroking himself, a jolt of pleasure racing through him with each moan, every whimper. When Pavle stilled, Chris held his breath and backed off, stroking Pavle long and firm until he gasped and cried out, coming hard and long, streaking heat all over Chris fingers, Pavle's release sending him over the edge.

"I…," Pavle whispered as Chris's mind, bathed in happiness, slowly returned to some sort of function.

He hurried to the bathroom and returned with a towel. After a quick wipe-up, Chris tugged off his shirt, stepped out of his pants, and climbed onto the bed, tugging Pavle to him. "You are stunning."

"What does mean?"

"Beautiful, radiant, amazing… all at the same time." Chris smiled and nestled his face in Pavle's hair. "I love you."

"Is that how you show it?" Pavle asked.

"Sometimes. Everyone shows they love someone differently. Some people…." Chris paused. "My mom told me that when she and my dad were dating, he used to give her flowers. Dad didn't have a lot of money, so he'd gather the flowers himself and bring her a bouquet." Chris snickered as he drew Pavle closer, gently rubbing his smooth belly. "One time he brought her flowers, and she sneezed all over the place. Turned out my dad said I love you with weeds."

Pavle chuckled.

"Saying I love you is all about doing something from the heart."

"Like when you cook for me?" Pavle asked, "Or hold me like this?"

"Yes. It's doing something you know the other person will like. Sometimes it's just lying still and quietly with someone, letting the spring breeze blow in the room." Chris quieted as his eyes drifted closed.

"Is how it was before... with Louis?" Pavle ghosted his fingers over Chris's arm.

"No. Louis was all about the sex. He didn't do grand gestures, unless you count stealing oranges and apples out of the cafeteria for me." Things had been very different then. He'd really thought he'd been in love with him, but it was something else. Chris could see that now. "It isn't the same."

Pavle rolled over. "Is that bad?"

"No. It's good actually. I've grown up, and what I want out of a relationship is a lot more than it was then." Chris sighed and grew quiet.

"What you want?" Pavle asked, and Chris rolled his eyes at himself. He should have expected that one.

"What's more important is what you want." Chris knew he was turning the tables, but really wanted to know. What surprised him was that Pavle didn't seem to have an answer.

"No one ask that before," Pavle said. "I want be happy. I know it simple, but that what I want. I come here to have chance to be success and good. So, I want that." Pavle kissed him gently, then closed his eyes... until his belly growled.

Chris chuckled and slowly slipped off the bed. He pulled on his clothes and waited for Pavle before taking his hand and leading him down the stairs to make some lunch. Chris tried not to think about exactly what Pavle would decide would make him happy, but hoped he was part of that mix.

# CHAPTER 8

"NANNA!" CHRIS called as he unlocked her front door and walked inside. Out of habit and caution, he looked around, his heart beating faster when he didn't hear her or Pavle.

Things had worked out remarkably well for the last two days. Pavle and Nanna kept each other company, and Chris came home from the station to a feast for the eyes in Pavle's smile and a feast for his belly, because the two of them had taken to cooking together.

A few of the guys had given him some shit for having a drug house right next door, but that had passed quickly when other excitement came up. Still, Chris looked at most of the guys he worked with differently now, thinking one of them might be a leak. He found himself locking his desk and guarding his work from prying eyes, and saw Briggs doing the same thing, while trying not to look like he was. Chris noticed, however, that the case files on his desk were old, cold cases rather than what he was currently working on.

This really sucked.

Just before he'd left, Briggs had stopped by his desk, making small talk and looking toward the conference room. Then Briggs walked away, and Chris finished up the report he was working on before joining Briggs behind closed doors.

"I hate this."

"So do I, but I think I might have found our problem. At least the source of the information." Briggs was dead serious. "The sheriff wants to talk to you. When you're in his office, take a close look around but don't look like you are. He wants a personal update. Apparently the FBI have been questioning how secure we are keeping our witnesses, and shocker of shockers, he's stood up for the department rather than rolling over like the spineless political snake he is." No animosity there… none at all.

"You don't think…?" Chris didn't dare finish the sentence.

"I can't think it. Everyone would say that I was biased, and it would become about me and him rather than the truth. Just look around. I have to go back to the motor pool and make sure everything is running right there. I'll call you tonight." Briggs had stomped out of the room, and Chris had gone to speak to the sheriff… and it took him mere seconds to spot the problem.

He'd been running through scenarios in his head ever since leaving the sheriff's office, and two hours on patrol and then coming to Nanna's hadn't dislodged an iota of worry and concern. Finding the house empty rather than the two of them sitting in the living room drinking tea only added to the tension that had been building for hours.

"Nanna! Pavle!"

No response.

Chris picked up the pace, hurrying through the main floor and ready to head upstairs, but he decided to try the backyard first.

"You are here," Pavle said to him as soon as he stepped out and into a riot of color. "We make pretty." He motioned throughout the yard, which had been cleaned up and planted with enough flowers to create a rainbow.

"He asked for plants, so I stopped at the nursery on my way over. Filled the trunk." Nanna chuckled from the patio chair in the shade. "It made him happy."

Pavle bounded over and handed him a huge bouquet of daffodils and tulips in one of Nanna's vases. "I pick for you." He smiled wide. "No weeds."

Chris couldn't help laughing.

"He insisted that he wanted to pick you flowers, so I told him to take some from the yard." Nanna had large patches of daffodils and tulips, though most were now in the vase.

"I show you," Pavle whispered. "I want you know."

Chris set the vase on the table. "I already knew. But thank you." Sometimes communication between the two of them could be slow and even difficult, but in this moment, everything was clear. He cupped Pavle's cheeks and kissed him gently. "Are you ready to go home? We have church in the morning."

"I made you some dinner to take home," Nanna said. "I'm going to eat and then go on to bed. It's been a busy day." She waved at them, and Chris let go of Pavle and kissed Nanna goodbye.

"I'll pull the car around the back, so meet me at the garage door." Chris went through the house and out to his car. He drove around to the back, and Pavle came out, carrying a small cooler bag. He locked the garage door and was getting into the car as Briggs called. Chris answered it through the car.

"It's me and Pavle. I just picked him up and am heading home." The car speakerphone picked up everything.

"Hello, Mr. Briggs," Pavle said politely.

"Hi, Pavle," Briggs began before immediately changing the subject. "Did you see what I was talking about?"

"Yeah. He has Post-it Notes all over his desk. I saw one with what had to be case notes and some with numbers. Who knows what he's jotting down and leaving lying around? That's a violation of so many statutes and procedures, it's ridiculous." He turned to Pavle. "What if he put notes about Pavle on one of those things?"

"Exactly. He jotted something down because he wanted to remember it, and then someone came in with roving eyes and found exactly what they were looking for. I even saw what looked like passwords, but I can't be sure."

Chris blew the air out of his lungs in exasperation. "What do we do?" It wasn't like they could go to the county board with this. They'd be kissing their jobs goodbye, and there was no guarantee that the board would take any action.

"Nothing for right now. You've seen it, and I've made sure some people I trust have seen it. Build a case and catch the bastard behind the leaks. If we can get him to spill about the source of his info, then we can go to the board, and they can't ignore that."

This was really sucky, but the sheriff was definitely connected. Though no one seemed to know how at this point.

"What about our friend in jail?"

Briggs chuckled. "The DA is throwing the book at him. Every charge they can think of, and the last time I spoke with him, he wasn't as smug as he was before."

"Do you think we might have a shot at getting Pavle's papers? Give the DA a good word if he cooperates. It will help the man he hurt a great deal."

Briggs hummed. "I'll ask. But what are you thinking? Good cop, bad cop type of thing?"

"No. I'm thinking, bad cop, bad cop, good cop. We rattle him so bad, he can't see straight. Then we get Pierre to come in to protect him from both of us. It'll be beautiful." Chris grinned. "We can talk about it later, once you talk to the DA and see if he'll help us."

"Consider it done first thing Monday." Briggs made a noise that sounded suspiciously like a yawn. "Get some rest. I'll call if I need or see anything."

Chris checked his rearview mirror. A car had been behind him for a while. He made a quick turn, and it made the turn as well, so Chris turned again, going down one of the little alleys around the old cemetery and then coming back out. The car didn't follow. He managed to buzz right across Hanover and continued on.

"What's going on?"

"Thought I was being followed," Chris said. "I wasn't. Should I check the car for any hitchhikers?"

"Had it done while you were on shift. It was clean," Briggs said. "We'll do it regularly just in case." He sighed. "I need to get some sleep. You have a good day off, and I'll see you on Monday, unless you need me before then." He hung up, and Chris did the same.


DINNER WAS quiet, and Chris wondered what was going through Pavle's mind. He had heard a lot in the car and had to have questions, but he'd said nothing for the longest time.

"Those people really try to help me? All of them?"

"Yes. We're helping other people too. No one works just one case at a time, but yeah. We try to help everyone we can and get the criminals and dangerous people off the streets. Briggs is one of the best."

Pavle nodded. "At home, we afraid of police. They always want something and are not so good." He took a bite of the flaky meat pie that Nanna had made, which was one of Chris's favorite meals of all time. "But you good and you help."

"That the only question you have?" Chris asked.

Pavle took another bite. "You really get my papers? They tell me I get back when I work off cost to get me here, but never give back." He set down his fork. "They mean, and I stupid. I should not let them take."

"They used you the same way they've used other people. The thing we have to do is get those papers so we can request for you to stay here."

"What is this bad cop, bad cop, good cop?"

Chris nodded. "It's a ploy in order to get Anthony scared enough to tell us where the documents are. We think he might have hidden them or has a safe-deposit box under a false name. The thing is, we won't know unless he tells us, so we have to make him."

"Oh, you make afraid." Pavle sniffed. "He do to me all the time. I afraid of him, always. He no feed me a lot. I get hungry and lay on the floor because I no can move. If I make happy, he give food and water. Sometimes, he give lots of food. Sometimes he leave me with nothing for days. I never know." He clenched his fist. "One time I no have food for whole week. Just water. I hurt bad." Pavle met his gaze, eyes hardening. "You scare him all want. He deserve. Make him wet self." The anger in Pavle's voice and the way he held Chris's gaze told Chris in no uncertain terms that Pavle was serious.

In Chris's view it was all right for Pavle to be angry. He'd been expecting it, actually. Pavle needed to come to grips with what was done to him, and being angry at the offender was perfectly natural. "I will do my best."

"Hang him up by nuts. Then maybe he get what deserve." Pavle smiled. "No, nuts too small. You hang by ears—they big enough." There was no joking in Pavle's voice at all. "I hate him. He nasty man. I hate them all." He pushed his chair away, left the table, and went through the back room. The door outside opened and closed.

Chris checked that Pavle was in the backyard and left him to himself for a few minutes, finishing dinner before going out to sit with Pavle. Chris didn't say anything. After a few minutes, he offered his hand, and Pavle slipped his fingers into it. That connection was all Chris needed to know that Pavle was going to be okay, eventually.

He sat back, held Pavle's hand, and looked up at the clouds that thickened and covered the sky. "It's going to rain."

"Yes. Good for flowers," he mumbled. The sky continued to darken as both night and the storm approached. Thunder rumbled in the distance, and still Pavle sat, staring upward.

"Come on. We need to go inside." Chris stood, gathered the cushions off the chairs, and carried them inside. Pavle sat still as the thunder grew louder and the first drops of rain hit the pavement. Chris came back out and took his hand once again, gently tugging Pavle to his feet. He led him into the house just as the sky opened up, drenching everything.

Pavle stood at the back windows, watching the rain, as Chris locked the door and set the cushions in the laundry room. Normally he'd have stored them in the garage, but there wasn't enough time. When he returned, Pavle hadn't moved from his spot. His hands were clenched and his expression as stormy as the weather outside.

"I hate him. Hate him…. I want him hurt… bad. I want someone punch him and kick him… hard… in nuts." Pavle shook with rage. "I want him never get out. Want people do to him like he did me." He quivered all over, fists at his side, hands shaking back and forth. "I want…."

"You're entitled to hate him," Chris said, but Pavle turned away. There was nothing he could do right now, and Pavle didn't seem to want company. Chris went into the living room and messaged Marie, who called him back. "Pavle is dealing with a lot of anger right now."

"Okay. I expected him to get there sooner or later. I'm sure Pavle's therapist will work through this with him."

"Great, because I don't know what to do." Chris leaned back, peering through the doorways. Pavle hadn't moved and was still as rigid and tense as when Chris left him.

"Be understanding. Part of this he has to work through himself. He had a lot of the person he was stripped away, and now he's trying to figure out who he is again," Marie explained.

They talked a little more and then ended the call. Chris really wasn't sure what to do, but went to sit with Pavle anyway. He hoped just being there would help. Chris took the chair near him, looking out the window as well, as water dripped off the roof. The downpour had softened to a light rain.

"I really hate him," Pavle whispered.

"It's okay to do that."

"He hurt me… a lot." At least Pavle had relaxed his hands and clasped them behind his back. "He deserve what he get." Pavle turned away from the window. "How do I stop this?" He placed his hand over his heart.

"Know that we're doing our best to make sure he gets what he deserves."

Pavle hmphed softly. "That what make me mad." He waved his hand. "Everyone else get to make him feel bad. I want do. I want hit him, take away food until he pass out on floor. I want to… I want it be me!" He turned away again.

"You want revenge," Chris supplied.

"Is that word?" When Chris nodded, Pavle continued. "Then I want mean revenge."

Chris took Pavle's hand. "The bad thing about revenge is that it makes you as bad as them." He hoped Pavle understood. "Hurting someone isn't the way to make yourself feel better, because when it's over, you'll hate what you did. You end up as dirty and ugly as they are."

"But I want—" Pavle's expression was almost frightening.

"I know you do. But do you really want to see him again? Do you want to look him in the eye and then hurt him?" Chris tugged Pavle to him. "Is that the kind of person you are? The kind you want to be?" Chris ran his thumb over Pavle's cheek, wiping away the tears that ran down.

"I never want to see again," Pavle said. "Still want hurt, but never want to see."

Chris hugged him, and Pavle clung and cried softly on Chris's shoulder, wetting his shirt. "It's okay."

"I all swirled up," Pavle said. Chris knew he meant mixed up, and he was allowed to be. "What I do?"

"You don't have to do anything right now." It was his and Briggs's job to handle Anthony and get what they needed from him. They had a plan, such as it was, and Chris would carry it through. "Come on. Let's go sit down for a while." The rain had ended and the last rays of the sun peeked under the edges of the clouds. This storm had passed, but Chris had no illusions that there weren't going to be more on the horizon. Sometimes he wished he knew which direction it would come from, but they were never predictable. That was the weird thing about storms—one could see them coming and still not be prepared.

CHRIS TOOK care of the dinner dishes some time later, and then he and Pavle went upstairs. It had been Chris's intention to take care of Pavle, but once they were in the bedroom with the door closed, Pavle pushed him back on the bed, his eyes a little wild. Chris was concerned for a few seconds, until Pavle climbed on top of him, pulled him upward by his shirt collar, and kissed him within an inch of his life. He could take a little roughness—he wasn't going to break—but it became clear that wasn't what this was. Pavle seemed to be asserting that he needed to be in charge, and Chris was more than happy to let Pavle do the driving.

One thing was for sure, Pavle certainly seemed eager, if a little clumsy, but that didn't matter at all. Chris held on for what turned out to be a wild, energetic ride that left both of them panting and huffing, sweaty, wrung out, and gasping for air on the damp sheets. Chris could only breathe and lie still for a long while. Then he got Pavle into the shower. With Pavle wrapped in a towel, Chris changed the bedding, and the two of them climbed into the crisp, freshly made bed, falling right to sleep and staying in bed a lot longer than Chris intended.

Breakfast the following morning consisted of two slices of toast that Chris grabbed and handed to Pavle on their way out to the car. They had ten minutes to get through town and to the church before the service started.

The room was quiet as they walked in and sat in one of the rear pews, but the music started a few minutes later. It had been quite a while since Chris had been to church, and he didn't know what to expect.

Pavle, on the other hand, seemed excited and swayed to the music, humming loudly because he didn't know the words, grinning the entire time.

The highlight of the service was Tyrone's sermon on helping others. "A kind act is like a ripple on the water. It gets bigger and spreads out. Sometimes it fades away. In fact, it does that most of the time. But other times it touches something unexpected." He paused for effect. "We all know about the house next door that is being torn down." A few "amens" scattered throughout the congregation. "That house was a den of iniquity. We've known that for a long time. But what we didn't know was that there were innocent people in there, victims. And we were able to help in our own way. Now, they don't know it, but they blessed us. Yes, my friends, it's good to be on the getting side of an act of kindness, but it feels so much better to be on the giving side. Let me tell you. There is nothing sweeter than knowing that you did something to help someone else. So, this week I'm going to task each and every one of you with a single act of kindness. Children, that can be helping Grandma, Grandpa, or one of your neighbors. I bet there are plenty of people who need help in their yards. And the rest of you, each of you knows someone in need. There are plenty in our community. And don't forget to watch for the opportunities you don't expect, because those are the ones that come from God."

Pavle turned to Chris. "He talked about me." He bit his lower lip as Chris nodded.

"Yes. It was very nice, and he said he was happy to have been able to help you." There was a lot more nuance in his words, but that was the real gist of it.

The service went on, and at the offering, Chris placed two twenties in the plate.

"Before I dismiss all of you, I want to welcome everyone to our spring potluck lunch in the park. The shelter is reserved, and the kids will have a place to play. All are welcome, so please stay for an afternoon of fellowship." He dismissed the congregation, and everyone stood to leave, talking as they went.

"Are you ready to go?" Chris asked. He didn't think staying was a great idea.

"We stay?" Pavle asked.

Chris hesitated before nodding. If that was what Pavle wanted, he was fine with it. He was concerned for Pavle's safety, but Pavle seemed so intent. Chris weighed the security implications with Pavle feeling locked away again. "For a little while. How about we hurry home so I can put something together? It will take some time for them to set up." And he wasn't going to arrive empty-handed.

On the way out, he shook hands with Tyrone, who smiled. "Are you staying?"

"Yes," Pavle said with delight. "We go home to get food." He smiled at Anika and Tyrone and Isaac, who hugged Pavle's leg. He knelt down and got a proper hug as well.

"Swing me?" Isaac asked.

"Yes. When I come back." Pavle practically vibrated as he left the church and hurried to the car. "What we make?"

"I have things for a salad. You'll have to help me cut things because we'll have to make it quickly." Chris took off and hurried to the house. They went through their arrival routine, and Chris got out the makings for salad. He and Pavle whipped it up in no time, and soon they were on their way back to the potluck. They parked and approached the pavilion as Tyrone extricated himself from the group to meet them.

"Welcome. I'm so glad you could join us." Tyrone turned to the group. "Everyone, this is Pavle and Chris. They joined us for services this morning. Please make them welcome." He smiled, and everyone stayed still, looking at both of them until one of the ladies broke the ice.

"I'm Wilma Carter," she said, extending her hand. She had graying hair and eyes as bright as the sun. She also had a presence about her that said no one messed with her without paying a price.

"It's nice to meet you. I'm Chris, and this is Pavle." They both shook her hand.

"It's wonderful of you to join us. You're a sheriff's deputy, correct?" Man, she was well informed. "And I'm so glad you could join us, both of you." She held Pavle's gaze.

Pavle smiled nervously and glanced at Chris as though he were wondering if he was going to get his hand back. Thankfully, Isaac ran up and barreled into Pavle's legs. "Hi, Isaac."

"Towers?" Isaac asked.

"We don't have the blocks here," Chris explained.

Isaac considered that for a few seconds and then pointed. Pavle nodded, and Isaac took him by the hand, leading him across to the playground.

"Deputy," Wilma began, and Chris wondered what was coming. "Excuse me for being suspicious… but….The police in this area haven't been helpful a lot of the time."

"Wilma, I don't blame you, and we need to change that." He looked around at a sea of faces all trying to seem as though they weren't watching the two of them. Ladies fussed with dishes and covers. Men stood in groups talking, or seeming to. "But… I'm a man who came because he was invited." He held her gaze right back. There was no way he was going to out-church her.

Her left eyebrow cocked upward. "You got guts."

"So do you. But mostly I have a stomach that's starting to wonder if my throat's been cut, and that pot-luck is looking real good." Chris grinned, and Wilma's lips turned upward.

"Don't go giving the man the third degree," Reverend Tyrone said. "We'll say grace in a few minutes, but I think you're needed to make sure everything is ready." He smiled gently, and Wilma nodded and returned to the tables, where she began marshalling the troops.

"I'm sorry. She can be a bit forceful," Tyrone explained.

Chris nodded. "I like her." He let his gaze travel to where Pavle played with Isaac and the other kids, pushing them on the swings at the moment.

Tyrone cleared his throat, and Chris returned his wandering attention back to where it belonged. "I spoke with the church council this week, and we agreed. Based on rumor and what we've seen and know happened, we believe Pavle was brought to this country and basically sold into slavery."

Chris swallowed at the word and nodded. It was a difficult thing to hear, especially given the company.

"We agreed that if Pavle wishes to return to his own country, then the church will pay for that to happen. He deserves to have the life he wants."

Chris was speechless as he felt the ground under him become a little less firm. "That's very generous of all of you." His world had suddenly shifted on its axis. Would Pavle want to return to Serbia now that he knew it was a viable option? He had to have family there still, and they didn't need to know anything about what had happened here. Pavle could start his life over surrounded by people who spoke the same language, in a place where Pavle understood the culture and customs. "Have you told him?"

"Not yet. I thought that maybe you could tell him. I understand that he has a number of court dates and most likely still has statements to give. But we wanted to give Pavle options once he's through with all that." Tyrone smiled, and Chris forced one that he hoped appeared genuine.

Chris nodded. "I'll pass the offer on to Pavle."

"Reverend," Wilma said as she approached. "We're ready."

He nodded, and Chris stepped back. The women called the children over from playing, and Pavle joined him. "We eat?"

"Yes. I'm hungry too."

They bowed their heads as Tyrone said a prayer, and then everyone lined up to eat. Chris and Pavle took a place at the back of the line and waited their turn.

Out of habit, Chris watched the crowd and the buildings around them, centering his attention on the now-empty house Pavle had been held in. The curtains in one of the upstairs rooms fluttered as though falling back into place. Chris continued watching as he pulled out his phone and barely waited for an answer.

"Briggs, was anyone supposed to be at the condemned house on West and A? I swear I just saw some movement inside."

"No. I'll have a couple cars head on over now and call Carlisle PD. We need to check it out."

Chris ended the call, and within thirty seconds, sirens sounded, getting closer. The group seemed to collectively tense as the cars pulled up.

"We may need to go right home, now." Chris was already moving Pavle toward the church and then inside. This had been a really bad idea. Going to church was one thing, but a potluck in an open park was quite another. In his desire to make Pavle happy, Chris might have stupidly taken a huge chance with his safety.

His phone beeped with a message from Red. *The house is empty and we don't see any sign of entry. It might have been a breeze.*

*Or whoever was in there had a key….* Chris offered. Seconds later his phone vibrated, and Chris answered it.

"I don't see where anyone has been here at all. There is a window that's loose, and it's letting the wind blow through," Red told him, and Chris sighed softly.

"Thanks. I saw what I thought was movement, and with Pavle and me at the church today, I...." He felt like such a rookie fool.

"It was good you called. The structure is very dangerous. Apparently the foundation is crumbling as badly as the rest of the place. Carter and I are heading out, but I wanted to get back to you right away. And thanks. It was a really dull day, and you provided some excitement. I'll inform Briggs."

"Thanks." Chris hung up and sighed. "It's okay."

"We go outside? I hungry." Pavle was already heading toward the door.

Chris followed. "Pavle, I'm sorry," he said, and Pavle paused with his hand on the doorknob. "Being here... I put you in danger." His heart still pounded a mile a minute.

"You thought you see someone?"

Chris nodded. "And we shouldn't be here. It's safer if we go home."

Pavle glared at him and then released the door, placing his hands on his hips, fire burning in his eyes. "No. I need get out, talk, maybe laugh. You come if want, but I no trade prison for prison." He stepped closer. "I no!" His lower lip quivered, and Chris wanted to try to explain to him that it was for a limited time, but Pavle was too angry. "You no wrap in wool and keep away from everything." Pavle turned. "I eat now." He yanked the door open and joined the others outside.

Chris shook his head. He only wanted to keep Pavle safe. He understood his frustration, but there were very nasty people looking for him.

"There you are," Reverend Tyrone said when they rejoined the others.

"Sorry."

"You missed the excitement," Tyrone explained.

"Yeah," one of the boys, about twelve or so, said. "The police were at the bad house." He pointed. "They're gone now." He raced back to the food table, and Tyrone rolled his eyes.

"You'd think the place housed buried treasure, as fascinated with it as some of the boys are. They want to go exploring because they think it will be an adventure." He shook his head. "Go on and eat before the teenagers vacuum up every scrap that's left."

"I will." Chris got a plate and filled it with some amazing-looking food. Pavle waved, and Chris sat down next to him. He wasn't sure if he was going to be welcome after Pavle's outburst, but he seemed to have said his piece.

"This Nadine and Gregory," Pavle said with a smile. "She make this." Pavle pointed to the macaroni salad. "It really good." He smiled and took another bite.

"I'm glad you like it," she said with a wide smile.

Pavle pointed, and Chris took a taste as well, nodding his agreement. It was really good, and unlike most things in Central PA, it wasn't sweet, but tangy with mustard.

Pavle chattered on with everyone around him. It must have been his true personality showing itself, and it was amazing to see. Isaac eventually pulled Pavle away to the swings as they finished eating, and a group of kids followed him like he had pockets overflowing with candy.

"They love him," Nadine said while Gregory watched Pavle and the kids. "Why don't you go over and watch them as well?" Nadine suggested.

Gregory finished eating and pulled himself up to his full six foot six or so, towering over everyone. He growled at the kids, and they giggle-screamed. Clearly it was a routine they were familiar with.

Pavle, on the other hand, paled and stood shaking like a leaf, looking blankly off into space.

Chris jumped up and ran to him. "It's okay. He's just playing."

"Oh… I think…." Pavle blinked and seemed to return to himself. "I was there again. I okay. I okay," he whispered. "He gone now."

"Come sit down?" Chris offered.

Pavle shook his head. "I stay. Need to put in past." He squared his shoulders and returned to gently pushing Isaac on the green-seated kiddie swing.

Sometimes the strength in Pavle blew him away. Chris returned to his plate, sitting diagonally across from Nadine.

"He's been through a lot. I know the look."

"Yeah, he has. The stories he could tell…. Let's just say I looked like a teenager last week." He smiled, and Nadine cackled. "Okay… well, maybe not that young."

"Like I said. I know the look. Each of my gray hairs has a name on it, and most of them are William, my brother." She turned to smile. "Gregory got fed up with the way things were and moved us here about five years ago. Philadelphia has its advantages, but we hoped that someplace smaller would be safer." She shrugged. "It's about the same, I guess."

"It always is." Chris raised his eyebrows, and Nadine smiled. "The grass is always greener until you get there and find out the green is just a bunch of weeds." He drank a huge gulp of lemonade. "And then sometimes, just maybe once in a blue moon, someone comes along and the grass turns out to be grass after all, thick and lush."

"I see." She nodded slowly. "I had that with Gregory… still do."

"I haven't before, and I keep wondering how long before it turns yellow." He continued the analogy because, hell, it seemed to be working.

"That's where the work comes in. If you want it to stay green, then you need to water it and fertilize it, mow it, and all that stuff. It requires care and hard work." She patted his hand. "But it's worth it…." Nadine rolled her eyes at Gregory. "Sometimes I wonder who the kids are in this family." Still, she turned, gave him a wink, and hurried over to where Gregory stood in the middle of a kiddie dust storm.

Pavle continued playing with Isaac until the picnic began to break up. Then Chris got his empty bowl and what was left of the dressing and packed them to take home.

"You know you're welcome here any time."

"Thank you. I'm sure Pavle and I will be back." It was never a bad thing to make new friends, and Pavle needed them. Heck, so did Chris. Chris shook Tyrone's hand, and Pavle did the same.

"I like it. I be back." Pavle grinned and nearly shook Tyrone's arm off in his excitement.

"I'm glad you got some happiness and hopefully a little peace of mind from the service."

"I think what got Pavle was the food and the children." Seeing him so happy warmed Chris's heart. "We need to go, but thank you all for everything." He met Tyrone's gaze. "I'm sure Pavle and I will be in touch."

It had been a special day, and he'd give a lot to see Pavle this happy. There were difficulties ahead—Chris knew that. But he'd take the happy times when he could get them.

# CHAPTER 9

"I NO want talk to more police," Pavle said Monday morning when Chris got him out of bed. He'd been sleeping hard and Chris hated to wake him, but he didn't have much choice.

"I know." He sat on the edge of the bed, smoothing the wayward wisps of hair off Pavle's forehead. "But the state police are coming in to talk to you. It's perfectly okay. Just tell them the same things you did to the FBI and everyone else." Hopefully they were running out of police departments to speak with. Of course, prosecutors and lawyers were the next step. Chris didn't bring all that up. One step at a time. "Try not to get upset."

"I will." Pavle lay back down, burying his face in the pillow. Chris gently rubbed his back. He was well aware that each time he told his story, Pavle relived the hardships all over again. "What about nutsack man?" Pavle had taken to calling Anthony that for some reason.

"While you talk to the state police, I'm going to talk to him and see if we can make some progress." Chris rubbed his hands together.

He turned his head to the side. "You break nose?" Pavle actually smiled at the notion.

"I won't actually hurt him, but if I can get him to wet himself, I'll consider it a success." Chris chuckled.

Pavle pushed back the covers, got out of bed, and padded his tight little naked butt into the bathroom. Chris had to remind himself that they needed to go to the station and that Briggs and the state police were not going to be happy if he decided to take Pavle back to bed and help him forget all about what was coming up… at least for a few hours.

"I'm going to get you something to eat. Don't take too long." Chris checked the clock, which read a little after seven, and went downstairs. He would give anything if he could take this burden off Pavle, but there was little he could do. It had often been said that the justice system was just as hard on victims as the actual criminals. Chris now understood why.

Pavle came down while Chris was plating the eggs. He added a piece of buttered toast and set the plate at what he had come to think of as Pavle's place. Then he handed him a glass of the grape juice he loved so much.

"I spoke with Reverend Tyrone yesterday." Chris had been running through what he should tell Pavle all night and figured it was best to just get it in the open. "He told me that the church has offered to pay for your trip back to Serbia, if you want to go home."

"Home?" Pavle asked.

"To Serbia. They will pay to send you there. You can't go until you're released, but if you want to go, you can." Chris had decided that he had to present the kind offer from the church, no matter how much he'd have liked to just keep quiet about it and have Pavle stay here with him. "You don't have to decide now."

"Okay." Pavle ate his eggs and drank his juice. Then he quietly took his dishes to the sink and headed to the back door. "I ready."

Chris finished getting ready, and they left the house in plenty of time to get them to the station on time.

Briggs met them in the back parking lot to escort Pavle inside. "Go in on your own. That way hopefully most people won't link you and Pavle together."

Chris agreed and entered using his usual entrance, saying good morning to people as he headed for his desk.

Briggs joined him a while later without Pavle. "He's with the state police now," he said softly.

"Did you speak with the DA?"

"Yes, and he said he'd take cooperation into consideration, but that's all. He isn't going to give us much to go on." Briggs sounded exasperated.

"Then let's see if we can talk to him again. Let's get Pierre and see if he'll help us out."

Briggs chuckled. "He's already on board. They're going to be with Pavle for a while, and I told the state officers to be gentle with him. They already have copies of Pavle's drawings."

"I wish I could be there with him."

"I know. But the best we can do for him right now is to find out where his papers are." Briggs motioned, and Pierre came over. "You ready?"

"You better believe it. Let's get over to the jail."

Since the office and the jail were on the same parcel of land, they walked over, showed ID, and requested that the prisoner they wanted be brought to an interrogation room.

"We intend to scare the piss out of him. We need a piece of information that will help one of his victims,"

Briggs explained, and the sergeant in charge nodded. "So we need a good room that's soundproof."

"Don't lay a hand on him," Sergeant Grill told them.

"Definitely not," Briggs answered, holding up his hands. "We just plan to scare him a little."

"Then use room two. Go on in. I'll have him brought down, and all you need to do is call when you're finished and we'll take him back to his cell." Grill was a good guy as far as Chris was concerned. He took his job seriously and felt strongly that the people in his charge were indeed innocent until convicted, and he felt that they should be safe while in his care. Grill unlocked the door, and he and Briggs went inside. Pierre would return a little later once he was needed.

Chris did his best to control his nerves and not pace, but still he jumped when the lock *thunk*ed and the door opened.

Harvey Anthony wasn't at all what he expected. The guy was maybe five foot three, with slight, almost delicate features. His eyes, however, betrayed his inner being, filling with fury at the sight of them.

"What do you want? I'm not talking to any of you." He sat down, head erect, uncowed by anything that had happened to him.

"You don't have to. We'll just stay here and stare at each other, then. I don't have anywhere to go, and neither does he. You aren't going anywhere in a hurry either. From the looks of things, the only place you're heading is to maximum security." Briggs smiled a little. "One-way trip." He crossed his arms over his chest, and Chris did the same, not saying a word, even though he wanted to charge forward and wring the scrawny asshole's neck.

Briggs said nothing else. Chris did the same, just staring. At first, he didn't think the tactic was going to work, but soon Anthony's leg bounced a little and his gaze shifted between them.

"Fucking hell, what do you want?" he finally asked.

"We have you on so many charges, it's unlikely you will ever breathe free air again. But you can do something for someone else." Briggs placed his hands on the edge of the table and leaned over it. "We want to know where you have Pavle's documents."

"I don't." His denial sounded feeble at best.

"We know you do, and we want to know where you have them hidden. They are of no use to you now and never will be again."

Anthony's lips curled upward. "That may be so, but I'm not saying anything. The little bitch can just rot in hell, but I'm not saying a word."

Briggs chuckled like an archvillain. "You've already told me plenty. See, we know a lot about you. We've already been through your safe-deposit boxes, and we've got what you tried to hide there. Those have already been confiscated." He curled his lips upward, and for a second, he looked like the Joker. "Those will never see the light of day again, except in a sheriff's sale for your victims." Briggs clicked his tongue. "Your wife and kids will get nothing, not that they want anything to do with you."

Anthony jumped to his feet, and Briggs leaped around, grabbed him by the collar, and pushed Anthony back into the chair. "Sit down."

"You leave them out of this!"

"Why? You didn't. You're not going to see your kids again. You've hurt them so much, they don't want to see you. You've hurt everyone who was ever important to you."

"Briggs," Chris said sharply. "You need to step out so I can talk to him." He banged his hand on the table, making Anthony jump. "This scum and I need to have a private conversation."

"What is this, some version of good cop, bad cop? You need to get yourself some new material." Anthony smirked and sat back in the seat, cuffed hands resting triumphantly on the table.

"No. See, we're both bad cops. I'd beat the shit out of you just for looking at me, and Chris here… he'd like nothing more than to bend you over this table and show you that turnabout is fair play." The look on Briggs's face was pure evil, but the beauty shone in the jab of fear that filled Anthony's gaze.

"You can't do that!"

"Wanna bet? This room is soundproof. It's where lawyers meet with their clients. No recording, no cameras, friends standing on the outside who aren't going to hear a thing." The back of Pierre's head of black hair filled the window in the door and didn't move. "There are no witnesses, so I think I'll let Chris have his way with you. Maybe he'll be able to demonstrate some of the things Pavle says you did to him." Briggs cocked his eyebrows.

"Fuck you!" Anthony challenged.

"No, babycakes," Chris said drolly. "You're going to experience exactly what you did to the people you enslaved." He lowered his arms and rubbed his hands together, stepped forward. "Get him out of that chair," Chris said to Briggs, then turned to Anthony. "Are you a virgin?" he asked as the fear spiked in Anthony's eyes. He looked from side to side like he was at a tennis match.

"There's no one coming to your rescue. You can either tell us what we want to know, or I'll let Chris have you like the little weaselly bitch you are." Briggs stepped in front of Chris to block him from Anthony. "You can either do this the easy way or the hard way."

"What's it to you? Why do you care about this guy?" Anthony asked. "He's just some kid from a shithole country who doesn't even speak English." His gaze continued darting around the room, fear rolling off him as Pierre stayed where he was and showed no sign of coming to his rescue.

"He happens to be a very kind person who you put through hell," Chris said, and then both of them stood still, staring once again.

"What will it be?" Briggs said. "Tell us what we want to know."

Anthony didn't talk, so Briggs shrugged and stepped aside. Chris stalked closer, wondering if Anthony was going to crack. Anthony bit his lips and indecision shone in his eyes. Chris had no intention of hurting him. Hell, the idea of touching this scum in any way turned his stomach, but he needed to help Pavle.

"So, let's get started." Chris turned to Briggs. "Did you bring the knife? That way I can cut his pants away before I—"

He didn't get a chance to finish. Anthony slid his chair backward and ended up falling back in an effort to get away. "I'll tell you whatever you want. Just keep him away from me."

Briggs righted the chair and slammed Anthony down into it again. "Where is the identification?"

"Safe-deposit box, Orrstown Bank, Camp Hill." He gasped.

"Is it under your name?" Briggs asked, and Anthony nodded. "Where is the key?"

Anthony's hands shook. "On my wife's key ring. Just keep him away from me." He slid back once again.

Chris knocked on the door, and Pierre opened it.

"We good?" Pierre asked.

Chris nodded and smiled before leaving the room, letting Briggs wrap things up. "Tell Grill he can take him back to his cell. We're through with the trash." He closed the door and finally felt like he could breathe. "We got what we needed."

"He told you?"

"Yes. I think he nearly pissed himself."

"So you didn't need me?" Pierre asked.

"Actually, you were perfect. All he saw was your head, and it made him think he wasn't going to get any help. It was awesome."

Pierre made a call, and Grill returned. Briggs exited the room, and Grill brought out Anthony to take him back to his cell. Anthony didn't seem particularly steady on his feet, and when he turned to look back, Chris met his gaze and he stumbled. Grill tugged him up, marching him down the hallway and away.

"Damn, that was masterful," Chris said. "You were amazing." With the tension gone, he sighed softly. "I can't wait to tell Pavle we got him."

Briggs phone chimed, and he checked the message. "Pavle is done. I need to go, and I'll take him to your grandmother's for the day. You go ahead and type up the request for a warrant, and we'll take it to the bank and see what's truly inside."

Chris hurried away as tension flowed out of him like water. One major hurdle managed.


PAVLE AND Nanna were waiting in the living room when Chris pulled up at the end of his shift. He went right inside, smiling as he handed Pavle his Serbian passport, along with his other documents. "We got them."

"Did you hang by ears?" Pavle asked, taking the documents with what looked like disbelief.

"No. I never touched him, and he didn't wet himself, but he was really scared." Chris sat down on the old sofa next to Pavle. "All I did was frighten him really badly. Briggs and Pierre were incredible, and we got him to say what we needed." He paused a second. "The man is a real ass and he was afraid."

"So what now?"

"We'll call Marie when we get home and tell her that we have it." The next step was for Pavle to decide what he wanted. Marie would know the ins and outs of exactly what they needed to do from here. But everything hinged on what Pavle decided to do.

"Okay." Pavle stood and hugged Nanna. "I come back tomorrow."

Chris hugged her as well and thanked her for her help. Then he took Pavle home and called Marie.

She was ecstatic. "I'll get all the paperwork started for an asylum hearing. Now that we have his identification and documents, it should be fairly easy. In the next couple of days, I'll bring things over, and we can review everything that Pavle can expect."

"Thank you," Chris said, then let Pavle talk to her while he made some dinner.

Pavle returned his phone and remained largely quiet. It worried him, but when Chris asked, Pavle simply shrugged. Chris gave him the privacy and time to think that he seemed to need, and spent much of the evening watching television with him. Pavle went up to bed early, and by the time Chris joined him, Pavle was already asleep. Chris slid under the covers, and Pavle immediately curled up next to him. He gently tugged Pavle closer, running his hands over his belly. Pavle mumbled softly in his sleep and didn't wake up.

Chris, however, couldn't sleep and spent hours staring at the ceiling. He'd hoped that Pavle would talk to him about what he wanted to do, but he hadn't said anything since Chris had told him about the church's offer. Chris didn't want to pressure him, but wondered if he should simply tell Pavle that he wanted him to stay. He sighed, closing his eyes for the millionth time, pushing that notion away. Chris had promised himself that he'd be better than the people who had hurt Pavle and that Pavle would be free to make his own decisions. No, he had to keep what he wanted to himself and let Pavle make up his own mind. Marie could explain his options to him, and when Pavle was ready to talk about it, Chris would be there.

Sometimes waiting was hell.

# CHAPTER 10

"Pavle, are you ready to go?" Chris asked. "We need to leave or we're going to be late."

"I ready," he said, and met Chris by the back door.

They were going to church again. Chris had been raised Catholic, but he hadn't been to a mass in years, and here he was, going to church for the second week in a row because Pavle was so excited about it.

"Okay, let's go." Chris opened the door, and they headed out.

"I see Marie yesterday," Pavle said as they rode together. "She come to Nanna's. Say police have what need." He turned to Chris. "They done."

"That's really good." At least he wasn't going to have to keep telling his same story over and over again, unless it was in court. "I'm so glad." He reached over, squeezing Pavle's hand. That was a huge worry off his mind. "We still need to be careful." The last week had been very quiet, which was a relief, though Chris remained vigilant.

He parked near the church, and they went inside. Nadine hurried up and asked if they wanted to sit with them. The church was fairly crowded that morning, so Chris was happy to have a seat. He and Pavle slipped into the pew as the music started and everyone stood for the first hymn.

The service was lively, with enthusiastic music and another great sermon. Tyrone didn't seem to be a "hell and brimstone" kind of guy, which was very refreshing. His messages seemed to focus around community and helping others, and Chris thought that was pretty cool.

"There will be refreshments in the park, presented by the women's circle." Tyrone ended the service, and everyone filed out.

"Can we go?" Pavle asked as Isaac raced up.

"Will you swing me?" he asked, and when Pavle turned to Chris, he could only sigh at his big beseeching eyes. This was not a good idea, and he didn't want a repeat of last week, but it was damned near impossible for him to say no to that look.

"Okay. We can stay for a little bit," he agreed, and Isaac pulled Pavle outside with him.

"Isaac, you be nice," Anika cautioned as she followed them.

Chris went as well and poured a glass of lemonade, then stood off to the side, watching as Pavle played with the children, laughing right along with them. It was hard to believe how far Pavle had come in a few weeks. He had started seeing the therapist more often this week and that was working out for him, or at least Pavle said it was.

"Have you figured out if he's the weeds or the grass?" Nadine asked, coming to stand next to him.

"Pavle? He's definitely the grass—green, lush, and perfect. But I don't know if I'm the grass for him." He could hope he was, but Chris honestly didn't know. He'd have liked to think he was more confident than that. Pavle would have to make a decision soon. Circumstances were going to dictate it.

Chris swiped at a buzzing bug near his ear. At least that's what he thought it was at first. Then he realized it was a bullet by the divot in the ground. "Nadine, get everyone inside and call the police. Right now." He turned, and to Nadine's credit, she was already moving as a second shot rang out.

Pandemonium broke out as everyone raced for the church at the same time. Screams reached Chris's ears, but he concentrated on where Pavle stood with little cover and Isaac crying in the swing. Chris raced toward Pavle and Isaac, pulled Isaac off the swing, and pushed both him and Pavle to the ground. "Take him, stay low. Move behind that rise over there, and stay put." He pressed Isaac into Pavle's arms and got them to some sort of safety as more shots rang out, followed by screams and panic.

He raced for cover and watched as Pavle held Isaac to him, both of them lying tightly to the ground behind the small grassy mound. They were safe, but for how long?

The shots were coming from the house right on the edge of the park. He had no idea how many shooters there were and he was pretty much pinned down.

Chris pulled his gun from under his jacket and called in to the station as he scanned for the gunman's location. Another shot echoed over the park, and Chris returned fire two times until flames shot through his upper chest. He fell forward, but lifted his head enough to see movement from the window where the gunman had been. He steadied his hand and fired twice right at the figure in the window before darkness overtook the edges of his sight. When no further shots were fired, he hoped he'd gotten the shooter.

"Get to the church… now. Stay low and go fast." Sirens were already sounding, and Chris watched for any additional movement as Isaac and Pavle hurried to the church, Pavle looking back toward him as he went.

Chris's shirt clung to him and darkened as he looked down at it. The realization that he'd been shot kicked in, but he didn't feel anything now. Chris knew it was bad, but his first thought was to make sure everyone else was safe. Thankfully, the park was now deserted and there were no bodies lying around. His strength flowed away, but he did his best to stay alert and on guard until teams of officers in blue swarmed the park and he collapsed to the ground.

Then Pavle was back with him, kneeling next to him.

"You were supposed to be inside," Chris scolded.

"I help you." Pavle rolled him over and pressed to his chest. "I helping."

"You always help me. You know that?" Chris tried to smile to make Pavle feel better, but all he could do was groan. His eyelids were too damned heavy. Chris placed his hand on top of Pavle's, just happy to touch him. "I need to sleep."

"No. Stay," Pavle told him. "You stay." Pavle's hand caressed Chris's cheek as he sighed a final time, giving up the battle against weakness and closing his eyes. "You stay," he heard Pavle say…

And then everything was quiet and dark.

DAMN IT all, he wished someone would shut off that infernal beeping. He was comfy, swimming through warm water, and wanted to stay there.

The beeping finally stopped and he settled into the water once again. Chris simply floated, with nowhere to go and in no particular direction. He lay still, arms out, eyes closed, chilling like he was on the world's best vacation ever.

The beeping started again, only this time getting louder. Off to his left. He wanted to swat at it, but his arm was too heavy and he couldn't lift it.

"Chris," a familiar voice said. "You need to come back. If you can hear me, follow my voice."

*Why? I like it here.*

"Follow my voice. I know you can hear me. Move your hand again, open your eyes. You've spent too damned much time in bed, and you need to wake up and stop being a layabout."

"Nanna?" he said, moving his lips, hoping sound came out.

The dream changed and the water drained away. Lights shone on the edge of his consciousness, but he didn't want to go. They dimmed then, and he sighed.

"Chris, come to me. Open your eyes."

He tried, but they didn't want to cooperate, and he figured he'd get some more rest. "Sleep."

"No. It's waking-up time. So open your eyes and look at me. You need to see the extra gray hair I have because of you."

"Nanna."

"See. You're almost there. Just try to open your eyes again."

Someone held his hand—Chris could feel it. He tried opening his eyes again, and this time they responded. The room was dark, with Nanna leaning over him. "Hi," he said even though his mouth was Sahara-dry.

"Sweet boy," she whispered. "You gave all of us a scare." She held his hand. "Your mom and dad were here, and they'll be back in a minute."

It took his eyes awhile to focus. "Where am I?"

"The hospital. You've been here for nearly a week. That guy who shot you nearly took you away from all of us."

He closed his eyes again. "But I'm alive?"

"Yes. You surprised all of them." She squeezed his hand.

"Is everyone else okay—Pavle, Isaac, the other people from the church?" He tried to make his mind remember all that happened.

"Everyone is fine. One person was hurt, but they're okay and much better already."

Chris sighed and relaxed. "Where is Pavle? Is he here?" Nearly his entire being cried out to know he was okay, to see so he knew for himself. "I need him."

Nanna shook his hand. "I don't understand. Pavle is leaving."

Chris opened his eyes once again. "Where is he going?"

"He's going home because he said you told him to."

Chris gasped and tried to get up. The beeping starting again.

"Just stay there. It's okay. You need to stay in bed."

"But Pavle is leaving?" Chris asked as people rushed into the room.

"You need to rest and calm down." The nurse leaned over him, pressing him back onto the mattress. "Please. You just came around, and things can be a little confusing. Relax and lie still. I don't want to have to give you anything to make sure you do." She checked things over. "Now lie quietly, and no getting up. I'll let the doctor know you're awake." She left the room again.

"Nanna, you have to get Pavle. I need to talk to him." Chris raised his hand, holding hers. "You have to. Don't let him leave." Fatigue set in, and as much as Chris wanted to stay awake, his eyelids became heavy, and he wondered if the nurse hadn't slipped something into his IV. "Please, Nanna."

"Just go to sleep." She patted his hand, and Chris lost the fight, slipping to sleep.

HE WOKE multiple times over the next few hours, each time hoping Pavle would be there.

"Mom, Dad," he said softly to his parents sitting by the bed, talking. "How are you?"

"Sweetheart, that's what we should be asking you." His mom smoothed his hair off his forehead, then picked up a cup of ice.

"I'm awake and alive, and from the fact that everything hurts, I must still have all my parts." Chris accepted an ice chip and swallowed gently, the pain diminishing as his throat remoisturized. "Thanks. How long have you and Dad been here?"

"We got here the day after the shooting, so six days, I guess."

Chris was a little surprised his father didn't go down to hours and minutes. He had this thing about giving precise answers to every question.

"I'm sorry I scared you." He accepted another ice chip as he processed what he'd just been told. *A week. I've been out of it an entire week.* "Where's Nanna?"

"We sent her home a little while ago. She's been here every day for hours, and she needs to get some rest," his father answered, barely looking up from the newspaper he was reading. "She said she'd be back in a few hours."

"Tracy, that's enough. Why don't you go down to the cafeteria and get yourself something to eat? You're getting grumpy, so maybe your blood sugar is low." She glared at him, and his dad stood and left the room without another word, for which Chris was grateful. "Are you still thirsty?"

"Yes. Can you see if I can have some juice or something?"

His mom left the room and returned with the doctor and a nurse, who pulled the curtain and folded back the covers.

"You're very lucky. We had to do a lot of work to put your insides back together." He checked the bandages and shone lights in his eyes. "It was very touch and go for a while. So you need to lie still and let yourself heal." He stopped fussing and stood near the foot of the bed. "You're going to be weak for some time as you heal, and we're going to be on the lookout for infection for a few more days, but so far you're doing very well."

"Okay." Chris somehow managed to get comfortable but kept glancing at the door.

"I'll be in to check on you again."

"Thank you, doctor," his mother said as his father returned.

Chris closed his eyes to rest and so no one would see how worried he was. Pavle was leaving because he didn't think Chris wanted him to stay? Chris used the quiet time to try to figure out how that could be. Yes, he hadn't tried to pressure Pavle. But maybe Pavle had interpreted Chris letting him make his own decision as Chris not wanting him here. God, this was a mess, and he was stuck here and couldn't move. Meanwhile, Pavle could be leaving the country and Chris would never see him again. The thought made him sick.

"Dad, I need your phone," he whispered.

"Yours is on the table right there," his dad said as he handed it to him.

Chris thumbed through the contacts. He called Nanna first, but she didn't answer, and then he tried Marie. Her call went to voicemail, and he left a message.

His hand was shaking at this point, and his dad gently took the phone. "You need to relax and rest. I'll turn on the television for you." He got the remote and found a rerun of *The Nanny*, keeping the volume low.

Chris ignored the television and closed his eyes once again. There was nothing more he could do at this time but try to sleep.


"CHRIS."

Nanna's voice worked its way into his dream. He opened his eyes and turned toward the sound.

"How do you feel?"

"Worried," he said softly.

"I know." She turned toward the door, and Pavle walked into the room, keeping his gaze on the floor.

As Pavle approached the bed, Chris lifted his arm. He took Pavle's hand, holding it firmly. "Nanna says you're leaving," he asked, and Pavle nodded. "Why?"

"You say I should go home?" Pavle whispered.

"No. I said you could go back if that was what you wanted." He held Pavle's hand more tightly. "I wanted you to decide what you wanted." His throat constricted, and he wasn't able to talk. "I don't want you to leave. You told me that you wanted home to be with me… at our house. I hope that's still what you want."

Pavle nodded. "But what you want?"

"I want you to stay," Chris answered simply. "I want you to live here with me because I love you." He tugged Pavle closer. "But you have to do what you want."

"Oh, for the love of Christ," Nanna groaned.

"Mother," his mom said, sounding scandalized.

Thankfully Nanna ignored her. "You both need to stop worrying about what the other wants and talk to each other." She turned to his parents. "Come on, you two. You can buy me lunch while these two talk." She took Chris's mom's hand and led her out of the room, with his father following.

"Come here," Chris whispered, and Pavle came closer. "I want you to stay here with me and live with me. That's what I want. I'm sorry I didn't just tell you that. But if you wanted to go back to Serbia, if you still do, I'll understand."

"But I no want to go. I think you want me go," Pavle groaned out as tears ran down his cheeks. "You no ask me to stay."

God, how could he have been so stupid? He should have known Pavle wasn't going to understand the nuance of what he'd been trying to say or that he'd been quiet to let him choose. "I didn't want you to think you had to." Chris blinked. "So, I want you to stay. Do you want to stay?"

Pavle sniffed. "Yes, I want stay." He leaned down, and Chris carefully folded his arms around Pavle's back.

"Then live with me and love me just as much as I love you." His own eyes filled with tears, and he held him as close as he dared. "Where have you been staying?"

"With me," Briggs said as he popped into the room. "Your grandmother got in touch with me, and she's pretty convincing. She said that you needed to see Pavle." He stood near the foot of the bed.

"Thank you." Chris lowered his arms, and Pavle straightened back up, wet patches shining on his cheeks, but Chris continued holding his hand.

"You need to thank him. The EMTs at the scene said that Pavle kept you from bleeding out. He saved your life." Even Briggs seemed to have been touched a little by Pavle's actions, judging by the hitch in his voice.

"What about the shooter?" Chris asked.

"You wounded him, and he's in custody. The FBI has him. Between Anthony, who is now scared for his life, and this guy, who the FBI has apparently been leaning on for a week, they've been rounding up suspects by the dozens."

"So do you think Pavle is safe now?" Chris squeezed his hand.

"Yes, I safe," Pavle said.

Briggs nodded. "We think so. They have much worse issues on their hands, and Pavle's testimony is much less important now that they have people from the inside who are talking."

Chris nodded, his eyes growing heavy once again as fatigue set in. "Did you find the leak?"

"Not yet, but I will." Briggs touched his other hand. "You concentrate on getting well. I'm going to need you back in top form as soon as possible." He smiled. "You did an amazing job, and I've pointed that out to the sheriff. Your quick action saved countless lives and got all those people out of danger." Briggs turned to Pavle. "And your quick action on him…. You both deserve a lot of credit for getting everyone out of that situation alive."

Pavle leaned over the bed, and Chris waited for him to get close enough before kissing him. "I kept looking for you," Chris whispered.

"I almost go."

Briggs stepped closer to the bed. "If you weren't hurt, I'd smack you. Both of you. Even I know that you need to talk, especially with your language issues." He rolled his eyes. "Don't make me get in the middle of things with you again. Romantic drama with my wife on occasion is about all I can take. I don't need you two adding to it."

"Did the church buy his ticket?"

Briggs shook his head. "Pavle was about to leave for Philadelphia in a few days, and they were going to process him through so that way we could figure out what was needed."

"Yeah. But he's staying. Right?" Chris looked at Pavle with a smile.

"Yes, I stay!" Pavle grinned brightly enough to light up the darkened room and send Chris's heart and empty belly fluttering.

"Then get with Marie and make sure she knows. We're going to have to apply for asylum." And God knew how much red tape that was going to involve.

"I tell her," Pavle said. "I happy now. I stay."

"Yes. You stay with me as soon as I get out of here. It's going to be a few days before they let me go." Chris rolled his head to look at Briggs. "Can he stay where he is for now?"

Briggs rolled his eyes. "I think my wife would file for divorce if I didn't agree. Apparently she and Pavle are redoing our backyard, and the two of them have bought out half a nursery." He sounded gruff, but Chris shared a smile with Pavle.

"Yard was ugly. No color. Now it pretty, and Gretchen can make pretty again next year." He looked at Briggs as though he were crazy. "Flowers are pretty."

"If you want to stay, you're going to need a job," Briggs offered, changing the subject, probably because Pavle was impossible to argue with.

"You can plant people's gardens. I bet there are a bunch of lawn and yard services who would love your talents." Pavle had a gift. "We'll worry about that once he gets asylum and then is able to get a green card." There were so many things that had to be hurdled before Pavle could legally work. Chris yawned as fatigue washed over him. He closed his eyes, still holding Pavle's hand, happy for the first time since he'd woken back up. Pavle wanted to stay. Now they had to make it happen.

# CHAPTER 11

IT TOOK longer than Chris expected before they allowed him to go home. He was already past stir-crazy after two days, and when they let him get up to use the bathroom after five days, it felt like a damned accomplishment. Two days later they finally discharged him. The doctor wanted to send him to a rehab facility, but Chris was having none of it. "I'm going home." And that was final.

His parents had returned to Florida a few days ago, and Chris was so grateful. They were scheduled to leave for a vacation in Europe in less than a week, and Chris told them to take it and have a good time.

"Who's going to take care of you?" his mother asked, and Chris told her that he was going to be fine with Pavle and Nanna.

When he was discharged, Nanna and Pavle picked him up at the hospital, with Nanna driving him home. He was never so happy to reach a destination in his life. Pavle helped him inside and got him settled on the sofa, with some drinks on the coffee table, pillows, and a blanket.

"Nanna staying here," Pavle explained, and Chris was already too tired to argue. He really was hoping for some time alone with Pavle, but he could also use some of Nanna's cooking.

Two days of spending his time on the sofa and his nights upstairs were much better. Pavle slept with him, and that made all the difference in the world.

"Marie come tomorrow," Pavle said once they were behind closed doors and Pavle had gotten him settled in bed.

"Is she going to help you stay?" Chris groaned as he shifted position in order to get comfortable. Pavle nodded. "That's good, then. You have your documents, that will help. She can tell us what we need to do." He slid over and patted the edge of the mattress so Pavle would sit. "Don't you be worried. Between her and me, and the other friends you have, we'll get this figured out."

"What if say I go?" he asked.

"Then we fight harder," Chris answered. "Because I'm not letting you go. I was so scared…." He ran his finger over Pavle's lower lip. "I thought, in the hospital when I woke up, that I wasn't going to see you again." His heart rate increased as he thought of how helpless he was.

"I no want go." Pavle leaned in, and Chris gently hugged him closer. "I never want to go. This home. You home."

Somehow Chris had to make sure it stayed that way.

"I'M SORRY I didn't get up to greet you," Chris said when Pavle let Marie in that afternoon. He'd heard the bell and thought it was part of his dream at first, the one where Pavle…. Chris pulled his mind out of his crotch and shifted his legs to hide the evidence of what thinking about Pavle did to him.

"I understand, and I'm happy that you're doing better." She shook his hand, and Chris motioned to the chair as he slid over to give Pavle some room to sit.

Nanna had gone back home, so it was just the two of them now. Chris really liked the alone time with Pavle. It was the best part about being home.

"So, what do you think about Pavle's chances?" Chris asked as Marie pulled papers out of her bag.

"Well, you found his documents, which is a huge hurdle. The next step is a petition for asylum, and that will involve a hearing unless it's rejected summarily." She sighed. "We have to prove a couple of things. First, we must be convincing that if Pavle returns home, he'll be persecuted."

"What mean?" Pavle asked, turning to him, already biting his lower lip.

"It means that if you go home, you'll be treated badly."

Pavle nodded until his head might fall off. "In Serbia, I shame." He shook until Chris gently stroked his back. "Gay, shame. They no understand I… what I…." He looked about ready to cry. "They might kill…."

"It's okay. Remember that we're doing this so you can stay." Chris needed to reassure Pavle as best he could, but this process was going to be painful. Most legal things were to some degree. "What else do we have to do?"

"I've looked up information on Serbia, and what Pavle says is backed up by case history and societal beliefs. But what I need from Pavle is a statement of what he believes will happen to him if he returns. They will take into account a sincere belief on the part of the petitioner. We also need people to speak on his behalf. I can do that, and so can you. But we need individuals respected in the community."

"Reverend Tyrone?" Pavle asked, and Chris nodded with a smile.

"That's a great idea. In this part of the country, having a reverend speak for you is probably a plus. We can ask him on Sunday." Hopefully Chris would be up to getting out of the house.

"Okay." Pavle turned back to Marie, who continued going through the application.

"I've done a number of these. I'll complete the form and run it past the department's legal counsel to make sure he thinks it will pass muster." She stood. "Is it okay if Pavle and I go into the kitchen? I can work with him to get this completed and his statement written."

"Sure. Pavle stayed with Briggs for a few days while I was in the hospital. Put him down to speak for Pavle as well. I'll ask him the next time he calls." This was suddenly very real for Chris. There was still the possibility that if they messed this up, Pavle could be sent home. He squeezed his hand, and Pavle leaned down for a kiss. "You sleep."

Chris had been doing so much of that lately, he was afraid he'd sleep through the rest of his damned life. He didn't argue, though, and Pavle went with Marie toward the other room. "Oh."

"Yes?" Marie said as she was about to pass through the door.

"Nanna, my grandmother, she can explain the kind of reception Pavle might receive if he were sent home. We also have more current immigrants who are willing to testify as well. We can call her, and I can arrange to bring her to the hearing. We'll find others and get a parade of people if we have to." Whatever it took.

Chris yawned. God, he hated being this damned weak, and sure as hell hoped his strength started coming back soon, especially when Pavle stood in the doorway, his small jeans-encased butt drawing Chris's gaze like a magnet. Damn it all, this was not the time to be having those kinds of thoughts. He turned away and laid his head back, closing his eyes.

"WE GO upstairs," Pavle said late in the evening a few days later. Chris had spent a lot of time sleeping and going from the bed to the sofa and was finally feeling stronger. Pavle and Marie had spent hours together, going over everything Pavle could expect, completing forms, and talking on the phone. They had what they needed, and she was going to run everything through the department lawyer before getting the petition submitted.

"I'm not really tired." Chris had napped and watched television for most of the damned day, so now he was wide awake and actually had some energy. He pushed the blankets away and slowly got to his feet. He moved carefully, checking for pain, but it was blessedly absent. "Tomorrow I have to go see the doctor, and hopefully the sutures can be removed." He still wasn't going to be able to go back to work for a few weeks.

"Come on. It time for bed." Pavle turned out the lights as Chris navigated the stairs.

He made it to the top and went to the bathroom to take care of business and brush his teeth. Then he got into bed, waiting while Pavle got ready.

The door opened and Pavle walked in, naked, and slipped under the sheets. In seconds, injury or not, Chris went from fatigued to raring to go, but it didn't last long. *Dammit.*

"You still not sleepy." Pavle grinned.

"I don't think I can do anything," Chris whispered.

"Maybe. But I do." Pavle slipped Chris's shorts down past his hips, fingers gliding over his length. All thoughts of pain, being tired, and anything else to do with his injury flew right out the window in two seconds flat. "You sexy man," Pavle whispered.

"So are you." Chris kissed Pavle, tasting his sweet lips as he slid his hand down his side and over his hip to cup a pert buttcheek. "So very sexy." Chris swallowed. "I love you." He drew Pavle into another kiss. "You take good care of me."

Pavle tightened his fingers, and Chris realized just how good of care Pavle was about to take. He groaned and tried not to tense up, but dammit, that was impossible. "You let me," Pavle whispered.

Chris managed to get both hands around Pavle, stroking down his back and over the curve of his butt. He had never been sure about touching him there, afraid it might bring up memories for Pavle that Chris didn't want surfacing when they were making love.

"Have question. We never…." Pavle paused and then patted a buttcheek. Chris didn't need an interpreter for that. "You no want to? Think I dirty."

And just like that, Chris realized there were other things they should have talked about.

"No. I didn't know how you would feel about it," he explained quickly. "I want you to be happy." He held Pavle tighter. "I can't do that now, but when I'm better, I want to do it with you. I want all of you, to be everything for you."

"You are. You home," Pavle said and kissed him harder. Chris's erection had faltered, but it returned with a vengeance as Pavle stroked him and then carefully slid down the bed.

Chris tried not to move. Pavle's lips closed around him, and Chris gasped, trying to hold any stress or pain at bay. Not that he felt anything other than Pavle's heated lips around his shaft. Excitement raced through him, and Chris panted, his eyes crossing. He lowered his gaze as Pavle's raised his, and their eyes met. He saw Pavle and only his Pavle, the man who held his heart. Chris guided Pavle upward until their lips met, a kiss searing its way past his heart to his soul. He knew in that instant that if Pavle left, he was never going to be same. Part of him would be missing.

"If you have to go, then I will go with you," Chris told Pavle. "I will dig ditches or raise vegetables for us to eat if I have to. But I won't let you go."

A tear slid down Pavle's cheek.

"I love you with all my heart." That was the simple truth, and it was so much more than sex and desire. He wanted Pavle with him for the rest of his life. "I want you to sleep next to me and be the first thing I see when I wake up. That's what I want, and if that's here or anywhere else, it doesn't matter."

"I love you too." Pavle ran his fingers through Chris's hair. "I want make love." He got out of bed, pulled at the drawer next to it, and put the lube and some condoms on top of it. "I want you to love me."

Just like that, there was no way for him to say no. Not that he had the willpower to turn down a request like that, one that matched his own heart and what every fiber of his being screamed at him to do.

Pavle climbed back on the bed, grabbed the lube, and used it to prepare himself. Chris wished he could see exactly what Pavle was doing, his cock throbbing as his imagination took over, his own fingers itching to experience the wet heat that awaited behind Pavle's back.

"God...." Chris swallowed hard, trying his wet his suddenly dry mouth.

He nearly came when Pavle rolled the condom down him. He had to think so many unsexy things he was probably never going to be able to be in the room with a salad again and not sport wood. But somehow he kept control of himself. Pavle lay down next to him, and Chris slowly rolled onto his side. Then Pavle guided him closer, pressing to him. Chris held the headboard, willing himself not to move as Pavle's body opened around him. He let go and slowly enfolded Pavle into his arms.

"Is this okay?" Chris whispered into his ear.

"This wonderful. This making love." Pavle pressed back, and Chris gasped as he was surrounded, pulled deeper, pleasure surging out of his control. Making love was one thing, but not being the one in control, having his pleasure at the discretion of someone else, was hot as hell. Pavle lightly rolled his hips, sliding along Chris's length, and Chris's eyes crossed. His hips ached to surge forward, but any sudden movement was out of the question.

"Be still," Pavle whispered, placing his hands on Chris's, holding Chris as he held Pavle. Pavle moved slowly, long and languidly, driving Chris out of his mind.

Chris slid his hands down Pavle's chest and belly until he found his cock. He closed his fingers around him. A shudder went through Pavle, and Chris groaned himself. He was already approaching the edge fast, his head feeling light, breath hitching and coming in gasps. This was mind-blowing, and Pavle seemed to know exactly what he wanted, speeding up just as Chris reached the precipice of desire. "Pavle, I…." Words failed as he tumbled into release, with Pavle following, his cock throbbing on Chris's hand, Pavle's gasps filling the room.

Pavle lay still, and Chris didn't have the energy to move. "You okay?" Pavle asked, and Chris chuckled.

"I'm more than okay. I think I'm either perfect or dead." He meant it as a joke, but Pavle scooted forward. Chris gasped as their bodies disconnected, and then Pavle turned over.

"Not dead," he said, "so, perfect." Pavle smiled, and Chris slid forward, kissing him.

"You're the one who's perfect." Now that he could see Pavle's dark brown eyes, he could get lost in them completely. Hell, he hoped he was never found. Chris yawned as fatigue caught up with him. He tried to stifle it and failed completely.

Chris got out of the bed and took care of the condom. Pavle helped him strip the sheets and remake the bed. Well, Pavle did most of the work, and then, exhausted and happy, they settled under the covers. Chris had just closed his eyes when his phone chimed. He picked it up, expecting a message from his mother. It was Briggs.

*Call me. Now.*

He pressed the number in his contacts and lay down, with Pavle snuggling next to him. "Hey, Briggs. I was going to call you."

"Yeah?"

"Would you be a witness to stand up for Pavle? We are applying for asylum for him."

Briggs sighed loudly enough that it sounded like wind through the phone. "Yes, I will, and that's good news. Do it fast. Apparently, our illustrious boss has figured out that the various law enforcement agencies have gotten what they needed from Pavle, so he called INS to inform them about his status. The asshole."

"Okay. Well, we've headed that off." Chris tried to sound positive for Pavle's sake, but that was a shitty thing to do after all Pavle had done.

"Let me know when the hearing is and I'll be there with bells on." Briggs hung up, and Chris messaged Marie to explain the urgency.

*The lawyer filed the papers just before the close of business*, Marie sent back.

Chris set his phone on the nightstand, wondering when this drama was going to end and he was going to have Pavle for always. Chris closed his eyes and hugged Pavle to him, telling him good night. All he got in response was a sleepy mumble, which was a relief. One of them might as well sleep, and this way, Chris could watch him all night long.

# CHAPTER 12

"YOU SUPPOSED to rest," Pavle scolded the way he had for the last week every time Chris tried to do anything.

"I need to move a little, and it's not like I'm going to haul a bunch of dirt in the yard." Chris sat in one of the outdoor chairs and put his feet up. Pavle got him a pillow and made sure his head was supported. "Marie just called, and tomorrow is your asylum hearing at the federal courthouse in Harrisburg. It's being heard by an immigration judge. Briggs, Marie, Pastor Tyrone, and myself are all going to speak for you. Nanna is going to come as well."

Pavle swallowed. "They all come?"

"Yes." Chris took Pavle's hand, drawing him closer. "Every single one of those people cares about you and wants to see you happy. They would all miss you if you left." He tugged Pavle closer. "I would miss you most of all because you have my heart."

"You have mine too," Pavle said rather haltingly. "I never think I...." He wiped his cheek. "I think, who would love me? Then I find answer." He pulled his chair over and sat next to Chris. "Thank you for love."

"It's easy to love you." Chris found it the simplest thing he'd ever done in his life. He leaned against Pavle's shoulder and listened as the breeze rustled the leaves that hung overhead.

A knock on the gate pulled Chris out of his happy thoughts, and Pavle got up to open it for Briggs. "Want drink?" Pavle asked.

"Water would be fine." Briggs approached, still in his uniform, and pulled up one of the other chairs. "I think we've finally pulled together a full picture of the shooting." He pulled out a notebook. "Your neighbor was anything but quiet while he was in jail, and apparently he passed the word around that his neighbor had some guest that he thought was Russian… or talked funny. He thinks it was Pavle who blew the whistle on him." Briggs shook his head. "The guy was stupid, but he had to blame it on someone else. We think it's possible that information got to our leak, but we aren't sure. What we are certain of is that Pavle was spotted at the church, and they kept watching it until he showed up again."

"Then why shoot me?" Chris asked.

"We don't know. I think he was trying to take you out before he got to Pavle." Briggs paused as Pavle returned, accompanied by ice clinking in the glasses. "Thank you."

"So, is that it?"

"I think so. I can't make any guarantees, and my advice is to be careful and watchful, but they would be stupid to try a second time. The entire department is on alert, and no one is happy that one of our own was shot." Briggs squeezed Chris's shoulder.

"Do we know who the informant is?"

"I think I do now, but it's going to be damned near impossible to prove it unless someone talks. With the FBI rounding up people, he's going to go as quiet as possible and stay that way."

"Unless we give him something too good to pass up," Chris offered.

Briggs huffed. "This isn't television, and we aren't going to put anyone in danger. But we will keep our eyes and ears open. Eventually they'll slip up and we'll have them." Briggs emptied his glass and set it on the table. He must have been thirsty. "I'll be here tomorrow to pick both of you up."

"What about Nanna?" Pavle asked, and Briggs agreed to give her a ride as well.

Briggs got up to leave, and Pavle walked him out. Chris closed his eyes and tried to think who the leak could possibly be. There were some deputies he didn't like and he wanted it to be them, but it could turn out to be just about anyone. Still, there had to be a way to figure it out. Hell, maybe it was easier than he thought.

"You sleep?" Pavle asked as he sat back down. "Marie coming."

"Okay." Chris opened his eyes but didn't move until he heard the doorbell. Then he went inside, letting Pavle get the door, and Marie joined them in the living room.

"I thought we should go over everything that will happen," Marie explained as Pavle sat next to her. Chris got comfortable in the chair next to his, listening as she took Pavle through the process step by step. "Just answer all of the judge's questions honestly." She went through what she thought would be asked. "I've done this many times, and the immigration lawyer will be there to represent you. These hearings are mostly procedural, and we have a really good case."

"Okay." Pavle held his hand as Marie went through the entire process a second time.

"Briggs is going to pick up all of us and bring us down there in the morning." They were both nervous, and holding Pavle's hand was the only thing that calmed him. There was a great deal riding on this hearing.

Marie stayed until Pavle felt more comfortable, and then she left them alone. Chris made dinner, and he and Pavle watched television before going up to bed, where Chris held Pavle all night. At times Pavle shook, and Chris held him tighter, trying not to let his own nerves show.


CHRIS NEVER liked going to court much. It was a lot of sitting around and waiting. Since they all were going to be speaking on Pavle's behalf, they sat outside the room, waiting for their case to be called and then for them to be asked to come in to speak. Pavle was inside with Marie and the attorney for quite a while, and then each of them was brought in.

When his turn came, Chris walked in, wearing his uniform, and took an oath to tell the truth before taking a seat behind the table in front of the room. The judge sat at the head. This wasn't a courtroom, per se, but it held the same weight in law.

"Mr. Kasun has plenty of support, it seems," Judge Vander-Lynde, according to the name plate in front of her, said.

"Yes, Pavle is quite a man." Chris met her gaze evenly as she folded her hands. "Pavle saved my life." Chris told her what happened at the church. "He helped control the bleeding until help arrived. I was told directly by the surgeon, as well as other doctors, that without him I would have bled out. I know that might be hearsay, but it's what I believe."

She made a few notes. "We understand from other witnesses that Mr. Kasun is very well thought of, and I take it you echo that sentiment."

Chris cleared his throat. "Yes, but…." He paused a second to clear his throat and continued. "Mr. Kasun, Pavle, is one of the most amazing people I have ever met in my life. Being well thought of is an understatement. I know the file in front of you explains how Pavle was brought here, but does it explain how he was freed?" He waited while the judge went through the pages. "After four years of being held and having his freedom ripped away, he was the one who sent a message for help." Chris explained how Pavle loosened the screws and threw the message. "The minister and his family—they found the note—are outside waiting to speak to you next. Pavle has a heart of gold and a backbone with more steel in it than I could ever hope for." He turned to Pavle and then back to the judge.

"So, you believe Mr. Kasun, if given the chance, will be a productive and useful member of society?"

"Yes. Pavle has been living with me for weeks now. He helps around the house. My garden has never looked better, and neither has my grandmother's. We have made initial inquiries with garden services, and they have shown interest in hiring him… once he's able to work, of course."

"Yes," Marie interjected. "As soon as he is able to work, we will help Pavle become self-sufficient."

The judge looked up from her notes. "You speak very passionately about Mr. Kasun, and that's to your and his credit." She turned to Marie. "Where will he reside? Do you have housing for him long-term?"

"Pavle is going to live with me," Chris said. "He and I have become very close. My grandmother has already been in to speak with you. She has become close to Pavle as well." He took a deep breath. "To be fully honest, I love Pavle. He makes me happy beyond words." Chris took a deep breath and held it. "I sincerely hope you grant him asylum. But as I told him the other night, if he has to go, then I'll go with him."

Judge Vander-Lynde cleared her throat. "I somehow don't think that's going to be necessary."

Reverend Tyrone came in and told her how Pavle had become a member of his church community and how the kids there loved him. He laid it on a little thick, and if the judge was surprised that Pavle attended a mostly black church, she didn't show it.

At the end, she closed her notes and took off her glasses, setting them on the table. "Few times in my career in this area of law have I had a petitioner with this many people not only willing to speak, but passionate and truly caring in their attitude. The law in this area is fairly clear, and I'm happy to say that all conditions have been met. Therefore, I am going to grant Mr. Kasun asylum in this country. I will request to see him in two months to review the case." She sighed. "Thank you all for your candor. You helped make my decision much easier." She stood, and they all did the same. The judge stepped out, and Chris smiled as they left the room as well.

"I stay," Pavle said, and was surrounded by everyone. Tyrone and Nanna each hugged him, as well as Marie and even Briggs. Pavle then stood next to Chris and slipped his arm around his waist.

"Well, what's the first thing you want to do now?" Marie asked.

"Eat," Pavle answered with a grin.

"Yes. Let's celebrate. Do you have time?" Chris asked Briggs, who nodded. "Then let's go to Café Belgie for lunch. This is worth doing up right."

Once they got to the car, Chris called ahead and then made a few other calls. Red and Terry were able to join them, and it became a regular party. It was about time they all had something to truly celebrate, and Pavle seemed happy as the center of attention.

"What's next?" Terry asked once they'd all placed their orders and Billy, the café's usual waiter, brought them drinks, worming the entire story of why they were there out of Pavle with the greatest of ease.

"A green card," Chris answered. "We need to start the process so he can stay here permanently. That takes time, but it's the next step." He drank his water, and Billy refilled the glasses and continued on to the other tables.

"I can help with that too," Marie offered.

"We'll write statements of support."

Pavle seemed a little overwhelmed. "I get job now?"

"Yes. The judge also approved a work permit, so you can get a job and earn your own money. I'll help you with that, and I'm sure Chris will as well."

Everything was falling into place, and Chris was thankful for each and every person sitting around the table.

The food came out, and it was amazing as usual. What Chris didn't expect was the cake that Billy brought out and set in the center of the table for dessert.

"A real celebration needs cake. I called over to A Slice of Heaven and asked them to send over one of Marcus's creations." He passed out plates and served up a slice for everyone.

"Thank you for come and for help. I no know what I do without. You help give me life and make me happy." Pavle stammered over a few words, but the meaning was clear. "I no think I have this life. You make possible." He leaned closer. "Especially Chris."

"You were always more than worthy." Chris stood and kissed Pavle gently. "You are the one who is amazing." He motioned to the others, and they all raised their glasses. "It is our pleasure to know you." And just like that, Chris's heart was full to overflowing. He had everything he could possibly want right next to him.

Pavle blushed, and Chris held his hand as he turned toward the guests. "I thank you all." He sat back down and leaned against Chris as though a little overwhelmed. It was going to take time for Pavle to fully realize just how much he was worth and how wonderful he was. Chris intended to make it his mission to see to it that happened.

Once the amazing meal was over, Chris paid the bill, and he and Pavle decided to walk home. It was only a few blocks. Nanna accepted a ride from Briggs, but saying goodbye took a while, as Pavle hugged and thanked each and every person there at least twice.

Then they did something they hadn't been able to do before: they walked through town, hand in hand, so Pavle could see everything and smell the roses in the courthouse square. They stopped in the candy store so Chris could buy Pavle everything that caught his fancy. Then they walked the final distance.

"Home," Pavle said as they stood outside the house. "This home."

"This is our home, and upstairs is our bed." Chris leaned closer for the last part. "You can build a life here with me."

Pavle grinned like a Cheshire cat. "I want to work with flowers like you say."

Chris could see him working to make the entire town pretty.

"Then we'll contact the places that were interested and see which one you think will make you happy." Chris closed the door behind them and sat down on the sofa to rest a little.

Pavle sat next to him, holding Chris's hand. "I get to choose, right?" Pavle threaded their fingers together, and Chris gazed into Pavle's brown eyes. He leaned closer until their lips met, knowing he'd spend the rest of his life thankful that in the end, Pavle had chosen him.

# EPILOGUE

"THE SNOW stopped," Pavle reported, letting the front window curtains fall back into place. "Do you want me to build a fire?"

"Please. That would be great," Chris said as he wheeled the vacuum cleaner into the room. He plugged it in and cleaned the carpet to get things ready for the party. It was nearly February, but in a way, it felt like Christmas. The holidays had been very hectic, and even though Chris had intended to have a party, it hadn't worked out, so he and Pavle had decided on an after-the-holidays party to get them through the doldrums of winter. "I brought wood in earlier to dry off. It's by the back door," he called over the whine of the motor, and Pavle hurried away.

Chris couldn't help watching him go. The months hadn't dulled his fascination with Pavle one little bit.

"Are you looking at my butt?" Pavle asked at the doorway.

"Yes," Chris answered honestly, then finished up the last of the vacuuming before putting the machine away. That was just one of the beauties of living with the man of your dreams. The other was sleeping with him every night and waking next to his smile and heat each morning.

Pavle was still chuckling when he came back in the room with wood and newspaper, and carefully laid a fire. Once he was done, he opened the flue and struck the match. The paper flamed and built, engulfing the wood and already filling the room with toasty warmth. Chris left Pavle to finish up, went to the kitchen, and put nibbles and munchies on the table in the center of the room.

"Hi, boys," Nanna called as she came in the front door. Chris hurried over to her, ready to scold for driving in this weather, but Richie came in behind her.

"Nanna," Pavle gleefully intoned, and he hurried over to kiss her cheek and share a hug. He shook hands with Richie and hung up their coats. "Did you bring them?"

"They're in the car, honey. Can you bring them in?"

Pavle hurried out the door, and Chris raised his eyebrows until Pavle returned with a casserole dish of ćevapi. The rich, savory scent was a clear giveaway.

"Just put them in the oven to keep them warm."

Pavle half skipped to the kitchen.

"Can I get you something to drink?" Chris asked as the doorbell rang.

"I can get what we need," Richie offered.

"Everything is in the dining room. Help yourself." Chris hurried to the door and ushered Marie in from the cold, along with Jordan and Pierre coming behind her, and Red and Terry as well. He took care of their coats, and the house filled with warmth and friendship.

"I love this idea for a party," Terry said. "No one has them this time of year, and we're all stuck inside because of the cold." He snagged some veggies on one of the small plates Chris had put out for munchies.

"The holidays are always so busy, and Pavle wanted to have a party himself after attending a few during the holidays. So this seemed like a good idea." Chris took Pavle's hand when he stood next to him, squeezing his fingers lightly until the doorbell sounded again.

"Anika, Reverend, please come in," Chris said as they stepped inside. She carried a plate of cookies, which Chris thanked her as he took.

"Are those your anise cookies?" Pavle asked, snagging the plate with a gleeful grin. They were his favorite.

"Of course they are," she said with an equally brilliant smile.

"Come on in. We have plenty to drink, and there are snacks and…." Pavle's voice faded as he led both of them away, and Chris answered the door yet again.

Within half an hour, the house was full, and Chris placed the last of the food on the dining room table. Everything was perfect, with candles and Nanna's borrowed trays and crystal bowls. Just as he finished, the doorbell rang once more. Chris answered it.

"Welcome, sheriff," Chris said as Briggs and his wife stepped inside.

"Interim sheriff," Briggs corrected, but he was clearly pleased. In the end, the sheriff had run unopposed, but revelations during the election period regarding lax handling of sensitive materials and the fact that his mismanagement of that information resulted in the compromising of witnesses had forced him to step down. "Thanks to you." Briggs grinned.

Chris colored and took their coats to cover it. He had provided some information that the sheriff had written down on his damned Post-it Notes. From there they had been able to trace who had been in his office when juicy, false gossip spread through the station. That had led to the exposure of their leak, as well as proof that the sheriff had been the inadvertent source of the leaked information. That sunk his battleship and he'd had to resign. A new election was set for the spring.

"We're so glad you could come," Chris said, motioning him and Gretchen into the living room. "The food is ready, so please help yourself." The others had already found the buffet, and most had already gotten plates. Chris stood back, making sure their guests had eaten before getting a plate of his own.

Conversation swirled around him and Pavle as they sat together on the sofa, talking, Chris's leg bouncing a little, until he could wait no longer. "I have an announcement." Chris opened the top drawer of the desk in the corner and pulled out an envelope. He glanced at Marie and then at Pavle. "Something very special came in the mail two days ago, and I wanted to give it to Pavle tonight. See, at some point, all of you had a hand in making this happen." Chris handed Pavle the envelope.

"What is this?" Pavle whispered, reading the sender, his body tensing.

"Honey, it's your green card." Chris waited for that to sink in and the smile to light his face, reaching all the way to his eyes.

"I am official. I am an American?" Pavle's hand shook.

"The next step is to apply for citizenship, which can take a while," Marie explained. "You have plenty of people to help you. But there won't be any more asylum hearings, and this says you're a permanent resident. You can work here."

"So I can stay?" he asked.

"Yes. You can stay," Marie told him. "God, I love it when I get to tell people that."

Chris left the room and hurried downstairs. He yanked open the second refrigerator and grabbed the bottle he'd had chilling. When he returned upstairs, he popped the champagne, and Richie passed out glasses so they could have a toast and truly celebrate and share in Pavle's unabashed joy.

THE PARTY continued well into the evening, with the last person leaving at eleven. Chris closed the door after saying good night to the last of their guests. Pavle sat in the living room, staring at the fire, holding the green card in his hand. "I can stay."

"Yes." Chris sat down next to him. "That card means that the country says you can stay here." He gently took it and set it on the table. "But this…." Chris reached into his pocket and pulled out a small box. "This says 'will you stay here with me forever and make this house… and me… your forever home?'" He opened the box, and Pavle gasped. "I don't want you to doubt in any way what you mean to me." Chris slid off the sofa, getting down on one knee. "Pavle, will you marry me?" He held up the ring and waited for an answer.

Pavle's lips moved, and he nodded. "I never thought this possible…. Yes… I will marry you."

Chris slid the gold band inset with diamonds onto Pavle's finger.

"But you were already and always my forever home." Pavle leaned forward and kissed Chris with enough heat to warm their hearts for the rest of their lives.

Keep reading for an excerpt from
*Fire and Obsidian*
by Andrew Grey

# CHAPTER 1

"THERE IS no such thing as a victimless crime," Mattias Dumont said as he slowly walked up the rows of tables filled with men and women in uniform. "And I hate thieves. They're selfish and care very little for others. They steal other people's hopes and dreams, their livelihoods. They're part of the reason all of us pay so much for insurance... because there is a victim for every crime. It's you, me, and everyone else. I really do hate theft, so it sucks that I'm so good at it."

He'd held the gaze of every person in the room up until that point. Then the deputies began looking at one another, some maybe even wondering if this was a test and they should take action.

A hand finally went up.

"Yes?"

"You're bullshitting us," the officer said. "You have to be."

Mattias came to a stop at the front of the room and leaned back slightly against the table. "The statute of limitations on all my crimes expired a few years ago, and if you look me up, you'll find next to nothing." Okay, now he was bragging a little, but that was the fun part for him.

"Because you did nothing," someone whispered from the back.

Mattias lifted his gaze from the front of the room to the back where a tall, broad-chested, jet-black-haired beauty stood, his arms folded over his suited chest. No uniform for this man. He was someone special. Mattias ignored the way his heart beat a little faster, the same way it had when he first touched an object he'd planned and studied for months to acquire. He'd always told himself he'd been in the acquisition business—he acquired things from their owners without their permission, often without their knowledge... sometimes for months.

Mattias kept his eye on Mr. Perfectly Pressed Suit as he continued his talk. "You won't find anything on me because I didn't get caught. Being a good thief isn't like in the movies. There's no *Ocean's Eleven*... or some such crap where you try to see who can pull off the biggest or the best heist. A cache of small gems that can easily be removed from their settings and would be hard to trace is perfection. I made a very good living under the radar. I didn't take the Hope Diamond, but I did steal from many people." To him it had been a profession, one that had gone sour over time.

"Prove it," Mr. Perfectly Pressed Suit said from the back.

The others in the room puffed out their chests, their police officer confidence kicking in.

"All right. Everyone stand up, please," Mattias said calmly. "Someone identify an object that you want me to take."

One of the officers held up a watch. It was plain and nothing that would ever have interested him during his career, but for demonstration purposes, it would do.

"Perfect. Put that back on, and I'll demonstrate. I'd like you all to stay standing as I attempt to take the watch." Mattias cleared his throat and pretended to think about how he was going to proceed. He wandered up and down each aisle, working his way over to the officer in question, who stood near the back, in the far aisle, with another officer in front and in back of him.

Mattias kept his expression neutral, as though he were concentrating, his gaze rarely wavering from his quarry. As he got closer, he nodded to the officer, whose gaze locked on to him. Mattias could almost feel his quarry's heart rate increase the closer he got. This man knew something was going to happen, and he was prepared for it. Mattias turned the corner, anticipation building in the room, so thick that he could taste it. Every eye was on either him or his quarry, which was fine. Mattias was calm and cool, no worries. As he got closer, his quarry's arm jittered slightly. Mattias watched it for a second and then lifted his head, meeting the gaze of the men and women around him. Passing by his quarry, Mattias smiled and continued back up to the front of the room.

"I still have the watch," the officer said, holding up his wrist, and the others in the room clapped.

"I guess you aren't as good as you thought."

Mattias waited until the ruckus and self-congratulations died down and they all turned back to him. He cleared his throat. "And you are?" It was best to confront this type of adversary head-on.

"Detective James Levinson. I'm working with the sheriff's department as a consultant on the robberies in the area." His steely gaze held Mattias's, and he didn't look away. It was a test of wills, and Mattias enjoyed it, especially from the stunning man who made his body temperature rise and his heart beat a little faster just from the intensity in his eyes. This was a man who didn't back down from a fight and who held tightly to his convictions. Mattias's lips curled upward. He got the feeling that this was also a man who never admitted he was wrong. Good. Mattias liked that.

Mattias was going to love making him eat his words.

"Let's see. Being a good thief is about doing what isn't expected." He reached into his pocket, pulled out a wallet, and opened it. "Pierre Ravelle." He smiled and held up the wallet. "I believe this is yours." The others in the room snickered as Pierre approached and accepted his wallet back. "No hard feelings," Mattias said as he handed it over.

Pierre blushed slightly and returned to his seat. "Come on, guys," Pierre said, to try to stop their razzing.

"Pierre isn't alone." Mattias began emptying the inner pockets of his jacket of their contents, including one more wallet, a pair of handcuffs, and a flashlight, as well as half a dozen other things. "Check to see what you're missing and come up to retrieve it in a moment," Mattias said, then slowly reached into an inner pocket, close to his body. He used his fingertips to pull out the service revolver and gently lay it on the table.

The room went silent, with each officer checking his belt.

"Detective Levinson, I believe this belongs to you." He kept the smile off his face, watching as the detective checked inside his coat and then stormed up, grabbed his revolver, checked it, and slipped it back into its holster.

"Now there are hard feelings," the detective whispered in a growl that under different circumstances would be sexy as all hell. Mattias swallowed hard and tried to put that voice and the way it sent a jolt of electricity running through him out of his mind.

"As I was saying," Mattias began after Detective Levinson had returned to his position, and the others had retrieved their lifted articles, "thieves rarely do what is expected." He once again leaned against the table in a relaxed stance. "I have done this same demonstration a number of times, and it's always the same. You're all trained and highly skilled police officers, so naturally you don't think you can be the victim of a crime, but anyone and everyone is vulnerable." He crossed his arms over his chest.

"How does this help us with this rash of robberies in the county?"

"Excellent question"—Mattias moved forward to see his name tag—"Deputy Brown. I will be working with each of you to try to learn how these thieves are operating, and then I will try to get into their heads to figure out where they might strike and how we as a department can get one step ahead of them."

"This little demonstration…," Detective Levinson said, clearly still smarting from Mattias's applied skill.

"It was to earn your trust and to prove to all of you that I am good at what I do and that I can help you. For the record, I am a thief, or I was, just like I told you. Now I run my own consulting company, and I work with law enforcement to catch and apprehend people like the man I used to be." Mattias held the edge of the table. "Do you have any questions?" A bunch of hands shot into the air. Mattias pointed to the man whose wallet he had taken.

"Deputy Pierre Ravelle," he said, identifying himself, then cleared his throat. "Will you be working directly with those of us on patrol?"

"I haven't been assigned to anyone specific yet. But the best thing you can do is keep your eyes open. Our thieves will be doing a number of things. They will be looking for victims and relatively easy, portable items."

Ravelle's hand went up again. "I work mostly in the courthouse...."

Mattias nodded. "You do realize that's a great place to case people. There are plenty of lawyers, and some of them represent well-to-do clients. They wear expensive watches, and clients may have jewelry and other items. It surprises me the number of people who actually overdress for court. Keep an eye out for people who shouldn't be there. I once cased a potential mark by posing as a garbage man. I hauled away their trash for a week. I learned plenty about them, and no one was the wiser. They had a security force, but they never looked twice at me." He raised his eyebrows as deputies nodded. "There are a million ways to hide in plain sight. Part of what we're going to do today is learn how to do some of that so you can learn the signs to look out for."

"What kind of signs?" a deputy asked.

"Not the ones you see on TV. There aren't going to be men hiding in TV repair vans or things like that. But a good way to be unobtrusive is as a painter. They wear coveralls, great for hiding tools and small pieces of equipment. They're covered in splotches, so people don't want to get too close in case they get paint on them. They're left alone and can often wander through a building or crowd unobstructed. If I were casing the courthouse and wanted to be unobtrusive, I'd dress as a lawyer."

"But everyone has to go through security," Deputy Ravelle said.

"Yes, they do. Remember that the building is public, though. You can restrict what people bring in, but not who can enter. Everyone has a right to access the government services inside the building, and if they're dressed as a lawyer, who is going to give them a second thought regarding wherever they go in the building?

Like I said, it isn't likely someone is going to be robbed in the courthouse, but it's a great place for people watching. So while they may be watching you, it's important that you are on the lookout for them."

With his introduction complete, Mattias started in on the meat of his presentation to give the deputies some things to watch out for. The session was scheduled to last all morning, and Mattias could readily admit that they were a good group. They listened, asked questions, and really seemed to want to know what could be done to stop what was happening. Of course, Mattias was keenly aware of the hard and continuous stare of Detective Levinson. He had given this type of presentation dozens of times and worked with a number of police organizations all over the country, but he'd never been as self-conscious as he was under the detective's gaze. Something about him got under Mattias's skin, and he had no idea what it was.

"Thank you all for your attention. I hope I get the chance to work with as many of you as possible," Mattias said at the end of his presentation.

The deputies stood, and many of them came forward to shake his hand, including Deputy Ravelle, which Mattias took as a good sign.

"That went well," he told himself as he gathered his things to leave the room.

"I don't know about that," Levinson said as he stalked up toward Mattias. "You could have gotten yourself shot in a room full of cops if anyone had caught you. How would that have gone over?"

"Detective Levinson, I can lift the gun out of a policeman's holster on a routine traffic stop if I want to, and there's little he can do about it." Mattias sat on the edge of the front table. "I have to give a demonstration in order for them to understand my capabilities, which I only gave them a glimpse of, and for them to understand how easy it is for thieves to get what they want, especially professional ones. And that's what you're dealing with, I'm pretty sure." He smiled. "Think of it as an attention-getter."

Detective Levinson rolled his eyes. "I think of it as a fox in the henhouse." He crossed his arms over his chest. "And don't think I won't be keeping an eye on you. I don't care what fancy title you give yourself or who hires you now. You're still a thief."

"Probably." Mattias leaned forward and waited until curiosity got the better of the detective and he lowered his arms. The he pressed something small and metal into Levinson's hand. "Maybe I can't help myself." He looked deeply into Levinson's dark brown eyes, which bordered on fathomless. "Maybe it's a compulsion. You know what that is, don't you?" He parted his lips, and damn it all to heaven if Levinson's eyes didn't widen and his breathing pick up a little at his taunt. For a second his upper lip quivered, desire flashing across his features, but it was quickly schooled away. Not that it mattered to Mattias—a second of true insight was worth more than hours of boring recon.

"That's…." Levinson paused as he raised his hand upward, scowling at the Swiss Army knife that rested there. "You better keep your son-of-a-bitch hands out of my pockets or so help me—"

A brisk knock on the door interrupted his tirade, and Mattias stepped back.

The door opened, and one of the deputies from the back of the class poked his head inside. "Sheriff Briggs wants to see both of you right now," he said.

Detective Levinson dropped his knife back into his pocket and straightened his suit. He turned toward the door and stopped. "You go first, where I can keep an eye on you," he growled.

Mattias chuckled softly, pulling the door open the rest of the way and leaving the room. There was something perversely rewarding about putting an otherwise-confident man just a little ill at ease. Hell, it could be downright fun, and as one of his foster mothers had told him years before, it was one of his supreme talents.

Mattias followed the deputy through the station and to the closed sheriff's office door. He knocked and received a call to come inside. "Good afternoon, Sheriff Briggs," Mattias said as he entered the office and sat in the far chair across the desk from him. "I believe congratulations are in order for your appointment." He reached out to shake his hand.

"Thanks. I'm still only temporarily appointed until the next election in November." Sheriff Briggs waited until Levinson came in, and had him close the door. "But that isn't going to happen unless we break up this ring of thieves that has been operating in the county. They've struck from Mechanicsburg to Carlisle to Camp Hill. Even the rural areas have been hit, which is why it's ended up on our plate. The various city departments have jurisdiction in their areas, but since this is bigger than any of them, they have all backed away and given us the go-ahead to take the entire case across the municipalities." He leaned forward, his hard gaze landing on both of them. "I brought you both in to work on this, find out what's going on, and bring them all in. Detective, you are the lead, and I'll have two of my best men working with you. Dumont, you are a consultant assigned to

Levinson and the team. You have a reputation for understanding criminals like the ones we're after."

"Yes," Mattias agreed softly, reaching for the file as the sheriff handed it over. Detective Levinson took it out of the sheriff's hand before he could, and Mattias stifled a groan. So this was how things were going to be, a pissing match? Well, he was more than up for it.

"Ravelle and Brown will be assigned to your team. They are both good deputies with a lot of experience, and they know their jobs and the county very well. If you need anything, you're to let me know, and I will allocate the necessary resources. This entire situation has much of the public on edge. The news media is calling it a crime spree, and every night there's some new story that is freaking people out. Homes have been entered during the day while people are home. They get in and out without being heard or seen, except by a few neighbors. The names of the people who might have seen them are in the file. Talk to them again, get whatever you can, and put these people out of business. And do it fast." His eyes blazed, and Mattias nodded.

"I'm sure the detective and I will work as quickly as we can." There was nothing else for him to add. Mattias had only seen the barest details up to this point. What he needed was a look at that file, and Levinson was holding it as though it were the Holy Grail.

"James," Briggs said as he turned to Levinson, "you need to work as a team. You've gotten good results much of the time, but you won't be able to solve this puzzle without teamwork and some help." He stood. "I brought both of you in because you are the best at what you do. Now I expect you to work together." He leaned forward. "And you will." There was no arguing with that tone.

Mattias had never worked with Sheriff Briggs before, but then, he often worked with new chiefs and departments. What was clear was that Sheriff Briggs and the detective had a history.

"I understand," James said, and the sheriff turned to Mattias. It was surprising how easily Mattias's brain glommed on to the detective's first name and held on to it.

"He's a good cop, but he tends to do things on his own, and that isn't what's needed here." Sheriff Briggs turned back to James. "Work together and get these people. There is way too much that's disappearing."

Mattias cleared his throat. "If I can ask, how long have you two known each other?" It was best if he knew what sort of political environment he was walking into.

"James and I went to the academy together in Philadelphia," Sheriff Briggs explained. "We were roommates for a while as well. Even then James was a superstar." He turned to James, and his expression softened. "You lived and breathed police work, always have. But I've come to realize that one of the keys to solving cases and getting convictions is teamwork." His expression grew pointed, and Mattias wondered what was behind the comment. He didn't dare ask, and filed it away for later. "I'd love to have you on my team here, but I can't do that if you won't work with them. We are too small a department for renegades." He drummed his fingers on the desk, and James and Mattias stood. Clearly they had received their orders and were being dismissed.

"You deserve this position, Solly, and I'll do everything I can to make sure you get elected," James said.

Mattias headed for the door, feeling a bit like an intruder on a private conversation. He opened the office door, stepped out, and closed it again. If they wanted to talk privately, that was their business.

"Mathias," one of the officers said, getting his attention.

"Mattias," he corrected as he stopped.

"Sorry. I'm Clay Brown, and you know Pierre. We've been assigned to the robbery team." Both men shook his hand, and Pierre patted him on the shoulder.

"No hard feelings, though maybe you could show me how you got my wallet so easily." He smiled and turned to Clay, who nodded. "The more we know about thieves and thieving, the more we can help people."

"Of course. I'll be happy to show you anything I can." They seemed like good enough guys. "Where are we working?"

"I got us a small room off the squad area. That way we can gather our information and keep it in one place. I got some boards and stuff so we can share ideas." They were both clearly excited to be working on this.

"This sort of thing can be tough to crack."

"We aren't afraid of hard work."

"Pierre and I are looking to advance, and we think this is a good way to do it." They opened the door and followed Mattias inside. The room itself was sparse, with serviceable furniture, a table that was scarred from years of use, and, as promised, whiteboards and a cork-board. "Where do we start?"

"James has the files, so we'll need to wait for him and then have a look, unless you guys know something?" Mattias asked, and they shrugged.

"No details, just rumors so far."

Clay snickered. "I have this theory that it's surfers who came in here to ride the waves on the creek off Children's Lake in Boiling Springs." He snickered, and Pierre rolled his eyes.

"Nice *Point Break* reference. You a Gary Bussey fan?"

They both shook their heads. "Keanu Reeves," they answered in unison, then laughed.

Well, that told him something interesting… very interesting. "He was hot then, wasn't he?"

The door opened and James strolled in, closing the door before dropping the file on the table with a paper smack. Pierre took it, and Mattias waited for James to say something. "What was hot?" James asked, slipping off his suit jacket.

"Well, actually, we were just musing on how hot a certain detective was in his suit and tie." Dang, it was fun to see James put off his game. "But now that you're here, we should get down to work." Mattias pulled out a chair and sat. "Let's go over the crimes, how they got in, what they took, time of day—all of that."

"It's in there," James sniped. "You can read as well as the rest of us."

"And we can either get to work or have a pissing contest," Mattias said. "Let's get to work. Lay out as much detail as we can and see if there are any patterns. If this is a small group of people, then there will be patterns of some sort. Thieves stick to what works—get the goods and move on. They don't reinvent the wheel for each heist. Like I said, this isn't an *Ocean's* movie." Mattias sat back, watching James as he pulled out the chair at the far end of the table, plopped into it, and reached for the file.

"Ravelle, would you do the honors?" James asked, handing him a red dry-erase marker.

Mattias lifted his messenger bag onto the table and pulled out a small laptop. He opened it and started entering the information into a spreadsheet as they wrote it on the board.

"What are you doing?" James asked.

"Going high-tech. If it's in here, we can search and rearrange it much more easily. I'm also hoping to see if the MO matches anyone I know." Mattias raised his eyebrows. "No loyalty among thieves and all that." He cocked what he hoped was a wicked grin and got back to work, listing the details as James and Clay called them out, going through nearly a dozen higher-end robberies.

ANDREW GREY is the author of more than one hundred works of Contemporary Gay Romantic fiction. After twenty-seven years in corporate America, he has now settled down in Central Pennsylvania with his husband of more than twenty-five years, Dominic, and his laptop. An interesting ménage. Andrew grew up in western Michigan with a father who loved to tell stories and a mother who loved to read them. Since then he has lived throughout the country and traveled throughout the world. He is a recipient of the RWA Centennial Award, has a master's degree from the University of Wisconsin–Milwaukee, and now writes full-time. Andrew's hobbies include collecting antiques, gardening, and leaving his dirty dishes anywhere but in the sink (particularly when writing). He considers himself blessed with an accepting family, fantastic friends, and the world's most supportive and loving partner. Andrew currently lives in beautiful, historic Carlisle, Pennsylvania.

Email: andrewgrey@comcast.net
Website: www.andrewgreybooks.com

Follow me on BookBub

A Carlisle Deputies Novel

Jordan Erichsohn suspects something is rotten about his boss, Judge Crawford. Unfortunately he has nowhere to turn and doubts anyone will believe his claims—least of all the handsome deputy, Pierre Ravelle, who has been assigned to protect the judge after he received threatening letters. The judge has a long reach, and if he finds out Jordan's turned on him, he might impede Jordan adopting his son, Jeremiah.

When Jordan can no longer stay silent, he gathers his courage and tells Pierre what he knows. To his surprise and relief, Pierre believes him, and Jordan finds an ally… and maybe more. Pierre vows to do what it takes to protect Jordan and Jeremiah and see justice done. He's willing to fight for the man he's growing to love and the family he's starting to think of as his own. But Crawford is a powerful and dangerous enemy, and he's not above ripping apart everything Jordan and Pierre are trying to build in order to save himself….

# www.dreamspinnerpress.com

A Carlisle Deputies Novel

The heat is growing from the inside, but danger is building on the outside.

Judge Andrew Phillips runs a tight ship in his courtroom. He's tough, and when he hands down a sentence, he expects to be obeyed. So when a fugitive named Harper escapes and threatens his life, Andrew isn't keen on twenty-four/seven protection… especially not from Deputy Clay Brown. They have a past, one that could cause problems in their careers.

But with Clay assigned to Andrew and the two of them together every minute, there's nowhere to hide from their attraction—or from the fact that there's much more than chemistry blooming between them. As the threat intensifies, Clay knows he'll do anything it takes to protect the people who are taking their places in his heart: Andrew and his young niece and nephew.

# www.dreamspinnerpress.com

# FIRE AND WATER

# ANDREW GREY

Carlisle Cops: Book One

Officer Red Markham knows about the ugly side of life after a car accident left him scarred and his parents dead. His job policing the streets of Carlisle, PA, only adds to the ugliness, and lately, drug overdoses have been on the rise. One afternoon, Red is dispatched to the local Y for a drowning accident involving a child. Arriving on site, he finds the boy rescued by lifeguard Terry Baumgartner. Of course, Red isn't surprised when gorgeous Terry won't give him and his ugly mug the time of day.

Overhearing one of the officer's comments about him being shallow opens Terry's eyes. Maybe he isn't as kindhearted as he always thought. His friend Julie suggests he help those less fortunate by delivering food to the elderly. On his route he meets outspoken Margie, a woman who says what's on her mind. Turns out, she's Officer Red's aunt.

Red and Terry's worlds collide as Red tries to track the source of the drugs and protect Terry from an ex-boyfriend who won't take no for an answer. Together they might discover a chance for more than they expected—if they can see beyond what's on the surface.

# www.dreamspinnerpress.com

FIRE AND ICE

ANDREW GREY

CARLISLE COPS

2

Carlisle Cops: Book Two

Carter Schunk is a dedicated police officer with a difficult past and a big heart. When he's called to a domestic disturbance, he finds a fatally injured woman, and a child, Alex, who is in desperate need of care. Child Services is called, and the last man on earth Carter wants to see walks through the door. Carter had a fling with Donald a year ago and found him as cold as ice since it ended.

Donald (Ice) Ickle has had a hard life he shares with no one, and he's closed his heart to all. It's partly to keep himself from getting hurt and partly the way he deals with a job he's good at, because he does what needs to be done without getting emotionally involved. When he meets Carter again, he maintains his usual distance, but Carter gets under his skin, and against his better judgment, Donald lets Carter guilt him into taking Alex when there isn't other foster care available. Carter even offers to help care for the boy.

Donald has a past he doesn't want to discuss with anyone, least of all Carter, who has his own past he'd just as soon keep to himself. But it's Alex's secrets that could either pull them together or rip them apart—secrets the boy isn't able to tell them and yet could be the key to happiness for all of them.

# www.dreamspinnerpress.com

# ALL FOR YOU

## ANDREW GREY

The only path to happiness is freedom: the freedom to live—and love—as the heart wants. Claiming that freedom will take all the courage one young man has… but he won't have to face it alone.

In small, conservative Sierra Pines, California, Reverend Gabriel is the law. His son, Willy, follows his dictates… until he meets a man in Sacramento, and then reunites with him in his hometown—right under his father's nose.

Reggie is Sierra Pines's newly appointed sheriff. His dedication to the job means not flaunting his sexuality, but when he sees Willy again, he can't escape the feeling that they're meant to be together. He'll keep Willy's secret until Willy is ready to let the world see who he really is. But if going up against the church and the townspeople isn't enough, the perils of the work Reggie loves so much might mean the end of their romance before it even gets off the ground….

# www.dreamspinnerpress.com